LORRAINE COVER

LIFE
After
LOVE

LIFE
After
LOVE

LORRAINE COVER

woodhall press

Woodhall Press | Norwalk, CT

woodhall press

Woodhall Press, 81 Old Saugatuck Road, Norwalk, CT 06855
WoodhallPress.com

Cover design: GetCovers.com
Layout artist: L.J. Mucci

Library of Congress Cataloging-in-Publication Data available

ISBN 978-1-954907-19-5   (paper: alk paper)
ISBN 978-1-954907-20-1   (electronic)

First Edition
Distributed by Independent Publishers Group
(800) 888-4741

Printed in the United States of America

This is a work of fiction. Names, characters, businesses, events, and inci-
dents are the products of the author's imagination. Any resemblance
to actual persons, living or dead, or actual events is purely coincidental.

To my husband, Randy: I would not be where I am today without your love and support all these years. You selflessly encouraged me to take the time to write, to see what I can do. I can never say thank you enough for helping me realize my dreams. I Love You!

ONE

Kate stares at the other side, the one without any wrinkles. She casts a gloomy look at the pillow not dented and the side of the bed not slept in. That was her husband's side of the bed. Correction: That was her *late* husband Peter's side of the bed. And it has been empty, just like her heart, for a long time now.

She shakes those thoughts away and quickly gets up. Although grief is her constant companion, she knows it does no good to dwell on the past that was and the future that could have been. She walks over and stands by the window, opening the curtains to let the sunlight in completely. She looks outside, and she is mesmerized by the beauty of nature. The sun is shining ever so brightly, and it contrasts beautifully against the clear blue sky. She forces herself to see the bright side of things and smiles to herself.

"Something wonderful is going to happen today!" Kate exclaims. She heads for the hallway to make her way to the kitchen. As is her custom, she stops at the first bedroom, her daughter's room. It's a

1

cheery room, white with touches of pink and yellow. Although it is empty, Kate still feels Chelsea's presence in the room.

Kate scans the room and remembers when she used to wake Chelsea up to get ready for school. Just like her, Chelsea would smile and get excited for the day. Peter would still be asleep, so Kate would have to remind Chelsea to be quiet. Kate looks at the room and takes in the way it has been decorated—pictures on the walls, paintings Chelsea had made herself, stuffed animals on the bed—and a wave of nostalgia hits her. For Kate, it isn't just a room but a lifetime of sweet, poignant memories.

Even now, it is still hard for Kate to believe that Chelsea is finishing her last year of college. She doesn't come home as much as she used to, and Kate certainly misses her daughter. But as a mother, she is happy. She is happy for her daughter and for the woman she has become. She is happy to see Chelsea become so courageous and independent. She is at peace knowing that her daughter is making a life for herself, filled with important things that matter to her, especially since Kate herself hasn't managed to do the same.

She takes one last look at the room before turning away and walking back toward the kitchen. Her journey to the past has only just begun, though, for the hallway is filled with family photos, reminders of the wonderful life she had lived with Peter and Chelsea. There are photographs from the time Chelsea was just a baby to her first days of school and beyond. There are birthday parties, holidays, and vacations. There is a noticeable decrease in the number of pictures toward the end. They didn't take as many after Peter died. There is also a noticeable decrease in Kate's appearance. She notices the once-vibrant smile that now looks forced. The glimmer in her eyes has faded. She catches a glimpse of herself in the mirror and asks, "What happened to you, Kate?"

It makes Kate's eyes glisten to remember how things were before Peter died. Some days, it is hard for her to look at these pictures. But even as she tears up, Kate is determined to make today the day she makes it through the day without mourning and grieving. And so, onward into the kitchen to make breakfast.

For as long as she can remember, Kate has been a morning person. She has been one of those people who gets excited about the new day and tries to get things done bright and early. She remembers waking up before her family and making breakfast for them. She loved doing that, and she tries to channel that same excitement today as she makes breakfast for herself and her two dogs, Sherlock and Molly.

However, it just isn't the same anymore. The eager, hungry faces are not at the kitchen table. Cooking one egg and a few slices of bacon isn't the same as seeing her family's excitement as she prepared their favorite dishes. Fortunately, her dogs like the food she makes for them and gobble up their breakfast quickly. They wag their tails happily as they eat, and she smiles at them. Kate fixes herself a breakfast sandwich and eats in silence.

Kate's ritual coffee, something to sip on as she plans her day, is next. She gets up from her comfy spot at the table and walks over to the cupboard. She looks over her eclectic selection of coffee mugs, fondly remembering how she acquired each one. In the far corner is an old Mother's Day gift, worn blue with white flowers that spell "BEST MOM." Next to it is a pinstriped New York Yankees mug, bought at the Yankee Stadium gift shop. Another, screaming "NEVER GIVE UP ON YOUR DREAMS," was given to Kate by her father right before he passed away.

She spots the mug she's looking for in the back, where it has sat forgotten like a childhood memory or a dream. It is a simple black mug that has faded over the years, but not enough to obscure the epigraph, written in bold white typewriter font: "WRITER." Kate remembers buying it on a family vacation to a movie studio when Chelsea was ten.

Kate always wanted to be a writer. She wanted to write and leave something behind. A published author, a screenwriter, a columnist; you name it and she wanted to become that. When she wrote, she gave life to her ideas and made simple words come alive. But her talent went unnoticed. She must have started and stopped hundreds of novels, poems, songs, even a screenplay, but has only just completed one project: a collection of steamy adult fiction short stories. She has a vivid imagination, and she wants to create stories that women would enjoy reading. Not exactly erotica or porn, but rather stories that are realistic and edgy enough to inspire her readers to want to have an amazing sex life.

Her sex life with Peter had been great, but considering he was her first and only lover, she couldn't help but feel there were things she didn't know. Of course, as she reads books and watches movies, she often discovers new details about what she had been missing out on in her sex life, but she doesn't let that bother her. Not that it matters much. There certainly isn't a line of men knocking on her door. The male attention she gets these days is limited to the creepy guy in the fish section of the supermarket. Thank goodness she doesn't like fish!

With her "WRITER" mug filled with fresh coffee, she turns on her computer. She feels motivated to start something new. Facebook is a nice place to start, she thinks, for she loves reading all the inspirational quotes, funny jokes, and memes. She likes watching videos of cute animals. A Brené Brown quote is first in her news feed:

"I think midlife is when the Universe gently places her hands upon your shoulders, pulls you close, and whispers in your ear: I'm not screwing around. It's time. All of this pretending and performing, these coping mechanisms that you've developed to protect yourself from feeling inadequate and getting hurt, has to go. Time is growing short. There are unexplored adventures ahead of you. You can't live the rest of your life worried about what other people think. You were born worthy of love and belonging. Courage and daring are coursing through you. You were made to love and love with your whole heart. It's time to show up and be seen."

Kate sits back, takes a sip of coffee and sighs, finding herself nodding in agreement with the words before her. She knows this, but the one question howling at her is, "How? How do I undo the past twenty—heck, forty—years of not feeling like I'm enough?"

Not wanting to deal with these feelings stirring inside, she logs out of Facebook and checks her email. The first message she looks for is headed, "God Wants You to Know." This daily newsletter is waiting in her inbox every morning without fail, with one inspiring message or another. These messages aren't just inspiring, though; they often seem tailored to Kate's experience on any given day. Today it's a familiar message. It reads, "Kate, God wants you to know that it is time to move into uncharted waters. If you want to do something you have never done before, you must do something you have never done before. If you want to go somewhere you have never gone before, you must go somewhere you have never gone before. You cannot do something new by doing old things. If you want your life to change, you have to change your life. So go ahead. It's safe. And it's also...about time."

This message speaks to Kate's soul. She knows it is time to move on, to stop toiling around the empty house and living in the past. She has all the signs of moving on, but figuring out how to take that elusive next step is a mystery. Then again, she knows it will require her to act and leave her comfort zone. In the past she had Peter to help her unfold her wings with love and assurance. Now she needs to find that strength on her own.

The next email causes Kate to sit up. It is from Award Publishers. It has been just about six months since she submitted her manuscript to the company. She wonders if this could be the catalyst to change the direction of her life. Is she finally going to become a published author? She doesn't need the money; Peter made sure she was financially set. But her soul needs her to see this through. It is all she wants.

Writing is her passion. It makes her come alive more than just about anything else. She knows that this is her life's purpose. Kate reaches for her wishbone necklace, rubs it with her thumb and forefinger, and opens the email. She sighs. It is a rejection letter. She forwards the email to G.

G, short for Giacomo, is her...well, it's hard to explain what G is to her. Kate Covington and G Amici have known each other since they were babies. It was because of Kate that G goes by the initial, not a full name. She couldn't say Giacomo; all she could get out was the sound *G*. Now, forty-seven years later, they remain friends, despite having lost touch for a decade or so after college. They reconnected when Chelsea went off to college, as she picked the school G went to for his undergrad degree. G has never been the marrying type, and the thought of having kids probably never crossed his mind, much to his Italian mother's dismay. When Peter died, G, now a powerhouse New York City attorney, reached out and helped Kate with legal procedures. Within a few months, she had come to rely on his friendship to chase away the sadness. He relishes that role.

They have absolutely nothing in common, yet they spend hours talking and laughing about anything and everything. They argue over just about anything and everything as well. Kate is a glass-half-full animal-welfare warrior; G is a jaded, skeptical, watch-your-back kind of guy. They have impassioned debates on a wide range of topics, but they never stay mad at each other for more than five minutes. That's because she feels comfortable around him. She knows that, despite his busy schedule, G would drop everything at a moment's notice if she was in need. Moreover, she provides him an escape from his work and the constant nagging of his mother to settle down. He is comfortable around her as well, for he can truly be himself with her.

The two of them are great friends, and they balance each other out. Whenever Kate has a story idea, she runs it by G. He is her sounding board. G is one of the few people who can make her laugh out loud. For her part, when G acts like a jerk and behaves too much like an attorney in his personal life, Kate is the one who reprimands him. She is the one who reminds him to call his mother and forgive her maternal nagging. Indeed, Kate thinks of G's mother as her own, since hers passed away when Kate was only twelve. Perhaps her reasons for reminding G to call his mother are a little selfish.

Those who know them notice a sexual tension or a spark between the two—and G's girlfriends would agree—but this is something both are quick to deny. So what if they text each other ten times a day, chat on the phone for hours, have inside jokes no one else understands, and are fiercely protective of the other? So what if they are always touching each other in some way? It could be a kiss on the cheek or even a quick peck on the lips, a slight graze of a hand or arm. They sit so close too. They can act like two six-year-olds, teens with a crush, or an old married couple.

Jarred back to reality by a ringing cell phone, Kate looks down to see a picture of G on the screen. The picture she uses is his professional picture for his law firm. His dark hair, dark eyes, and tanned skin are accentuated in his dark pinstripe suit. His smile radiates confidence. She answers the phone, sure of what he is going to say.

"Hey," she musters.

"At least you finally heard something back," he says.

"I knew you were going to say that. Did you read the reason they rejected it?" Kate inquires.

"No, what did they say?"

"They felt it didn't fit the type of fiction they publish," she says, sounding insulted.

"Maybe they aren't into steamy novels?"

"G, all they publish is steamy adult fiction, so that means they just didn't think my work was steamy enough. You thought it was, right?" Her desire to hear positive feedback is not subtle.

"Well, yes, I mean, considering your, um, limited experience, it was steamy...ish." G says, holding his breath.

"I thought you said you liked it."

And there it is: the moment he was hoping to avoid. Why didn't this publisher accept her book and save him the headache? He said, "I did! I liked your stories; it's the perfect example of writing what you know. Not quite *50 Shades of Grey*, more like *50 Shades of Beige*."

The moment the words leave his mouth, he knows he has made a mistake and wants to take them back. He knows he needs to think fast. Recovering from the shock of disappointment, Kate starts to regain the relentless spirit she only ever seems to summon when dealing with G.

"Why don't you send it to a different kind of publisher?" he asks. He's only digging a deeper hole. How can one woman fluster him so easily and so often?

The deafening silence on the other end only makes it worse. He wants to be her biggest supporter, the rock on which she leans, not the one to tell her the bad news. Breaking the silence, G proudly states, "Hey, no one wants you to succeed more than I do. I get 40 percent of the profits!"

"You get squat—other than my undying gratitude." Kate says, without hiding her laughter. As always, G knows the right thing to say at the right time. He knows how to cheer her up.

"I guess I thought this was the time it was going to happen," she sighs wistfully. In her head, Kate looks back over the past thirty years of her life, during which she pushed aside her desire to be a published author and justified putting it on hold. First, to get married, then to raise a child, then to open a business. She thought her time had finally come...but no.

"It will happen. Don't worry," says G, interrupting her wallowing. "Hey, before I forget, keep the 25th open for my birthday dinner. It's at Il Tulipano. Make sure you get me a good gift."

She rolls her eyes in response. That's G, caring and sweet one second, selfish and insensitive the next.

"Already have it on the calendar," she jabs. "Your mom called me the other day. I put in the order for your Porsche, puke green was the color you like, right? Hopefully it gets here in time."

Kate is about to continue when she hears a feminine voice in the background. It sounds sleepy and slightly agitated. Kate surmises that G must have had a lady friend spend the night—and that said lady friend doesn't take well to playfully combative 7:30 a.m. phone calls. Kate is used to it. More often than not, early in the morning or late at night, G has a woman nearby.

The fact is, G has an abundance of women chasing him. Kate understands why: The man is handsome, smart, rich, and funny. She imagines he's also a good lover, maybe even a great lover. The few times they have danced together, she enjoyed being so close to him, feeling his arms around her. And she has that one kiss to remember. Too bad he doesn't know it was her in that closet with him at the graduation party. Now is not time to reminisce about all the close calls and missed opportunities. Kate smiles, remembering the time she dreamt she was in G's bedroom, him just coming out of the shower. She gets up, approaches him, removes his towel, and proceeds to give him a blow job. The next day she somehow summoned the courage to tell him, shy to say "blow job" so instead saying a "BJ." He laughed then, but later admitted that he'd had a hard-on the rest of the day after she told him.

For some reason, his latest girlfriend, Alexandra, irritates Kate more than most.

"Oh, did I interrupt something?" Kate deadpans before adding, "Is that Alexandra? Or someone else?" She immediately wishes she could take that last barb back.

"I heard that!" the woman yells loudly enough for Kate to hear, and at once Kate ceases to feel bad for her. In fact, knowing she has annoyed Alexandra makes Kate smile.

G sighs and, rather than waiting for him to say something, Kate declares, "I have to run; talk to you later." She knows full well that he will bring it up later, just like always. And she'll be ready with a list of what's wrong with Alexandra. He'll agree, and that will be the end of her. Kate hangs up before G has a chance to say anything.

On the other end of the phone line, Alexandra is not amused. "Honestly, G, you talk to Kate more than you talk to me," she complains.

G sighs again, realizing this is about the point in the relationship where he moves on and finds the next woman. In time, all of them become whiny. He hates how the women he dates come to nag or expect commitment. That's his cue to leave the relationship, and he knows it has to be done here as well.

Kate, however, has no idea what is unfolding between G and Alexandra. She goes about her routine, and after letting the pups back in the house, she gives them the rundown of her day. "Okay, puppers," she begins, "I have some errands to run, and I am going to the animal shelter to take some friends for a walk. I'll be back in a few hours. Be good!"

They don't question her. They're happy to be loved and get a belly rub. How nice!

It's a twenty-minute drive to the shelter, and thoughts of her writing fill her head. "Well, it sounded steamy to me when I wrote it," she says out loud. And that's when it hits her—her random stories of random sex between strangers are not steamy. Just because the stories have sex in them doesn't mean they are interesting to read. Just because deep down she wants to have a steamy sex life, it doesn't mean she can create one on paper. Now what? To distract herself from the rejection letter and the realization that she has no business writing about steamy sex, Kate turns on the radio with the intent to blast some music. The receiver, however, is tuned to the Inspiration station, whose thirty-minute broadcasts never fail to uplift. Nice timing to have that station on, she thought, especially so after hearing what the speaker said:

"There will be plenty of opportunities to get discouraged, to lose your passion and think that it's not meant to be. But if you're going to reach your destiny, you have to have a made-up mind. If you give up after the first time, or the fifth time or the thirtieth time, what that really means is you didn't want it bad enough. There should be something that you're believing for that you are relentless. You are not moved by how impossible it looks, you're not discouraged by how long it's taking, you don't give up because people told you no, your attitude is: 'If I have to believe my whole life, I am not going to stop believing, I am not going to take no for an answer, I'm not going to settle for mediocrity.'"

She smiles and sighs. "Thanks, Universe," she says out loud. "You certainly know how to pick me up, dust me off, and get me going again." She has always been a believer in a higher spirit that runs through all of us. That belief has given her strength, especially after Peter's death, and she needs strength to keep going. She finds comfort in the slightest of signs, reassuring her that everything is going to be all right.

Inspired by what she has just heard; her mind goes into fourth gear.

"Siri, call Claudia."

Claudia is Kate's best friend. The two met when their daughters became fast friends in kindergarten, the mothers following their lead. Claudia was a single mom at that time, having just lost her husband to cancer. She was also a career-oriented woman who had done a lot in a short time span. She liked to travel and explore. She was a Broadway fanatic. Most importantly, she was one of the most fun people to be around. When Peter died, Claudia was a good friend to lean on and learn from.

"Hey, babes! What's up?" Kate never tires of hearing Claudia's usual cheery spirit.

"Hey, I've been thinking, and I think I need to have sex," Kate blurts. "I need your help."

Kate hears a loud crash and imagines it's Claudia either falling over or dropping her phone. In any case, she immediately realizes how shocking her request must sound. Although not usually surprised by much, Claudia is seriously taken aback, and not sure how to respond.

"Well, I...um...I'm showing a property at 11, but I can clear my schedule for the afternoon," she quips.

In an effort to right the wrong conversation, Kate reassures her friend. "You know I think you're hot, but I was actually thinking about a one-night stand—hot, steamy sex with some random guy."

Sounding relieved, Claudia asks, "Okay, don't get me wrong, because I am happy to hear that you want to get back out there, but where is this coming from all of a sudden? I haven't been able to get you out of the house on a weekend, or a weeknight for that matter."

"I got a rejection letter for my steamy adult fiction book."

"Aww, I'm sorry."

"They said it wasn't steamy. I was talking to G this morning, and he now admits it was my level of steamy, whatever that means. And he reminded me of the saying 'Write what you know.'"

"Wow, G was actually helpful. Okay, okay, let me think. You want to go out this weekend?"

"Well, I have an idea, and I need you to say yes, you'll come with me," Kate begins.

"Of course, babes. You say where and when, and I'll be there!"

"I was hoping you'd say that! I thought a cruise would be a good way to meet someone. Pretty safe, lots of people."

"Oh, I love that!" Claudia immediately begins planning everything in her head. She will make sure this cruise is exactly what her friend wants. Kate can almost hear the clicking of Claudia's keyboard as she starts searching for cruises. "Where to? Bahamas? Caribbean? There are tons leaving from New York pretty much every day."

A control freak at heart, Kate won't risk a cruise from New York. "I was thinking a little farther. Someplace where I would pretty much be guaranteed that, you know, the guy I you-know-what with...well...I wouldn't run in to him again."

Claudia wonders what her friend has in mind and lets out a long, questioning *o-ka-a-a-ay* in response.

"Let me plan it!" Kate says. "It will be amazing! Do you speak any other language?"

Unknown to Claudia, Kate has a comprehensive wish list of places to visit: England, Italy, Ireland, Scotland—there are just so many choices. She speaks some Spanish, and since Claudia grew up in England, she decides to look for a cruise from England that stops perhaps in a Spanish port. The only other person that Kate knows who is more traveled than Claudia is G, so Kate decides to tell him her plan.

With no time to wait for a text reply, Kate calls G, and he answers right away.

"So have you bounced back from this morning?" he asks.

"I did!" Kate answers, rambling. "So much so that I have had a brilliant idea! Claudia and I are going on a cruise, from London, that stops at some port in Spain—"

"Am I invited?" G interrupts.

A dozen images race through Kate's mind: Her and G on a cruise, alone in a crowd of strangers, romantic dinners...but she quickly quashes that thought. Instead she says, "No, because you would cramp my style."

"Oh, really?"

"Yes. Now don't faint, but you are right about something."

"Holy crap!" G says with exaggerated excitement. "What did you say? I need to mark this occasion."

"Very funny. I do write what I know, so if I want to write steamy adult fiction, then I'd better experience some," Kate tells him.

"I'm not sure I like where this is going." G says, sounding confused.

"So, what is the safest, most likely place to have a one-night stand?"

"I don't know the statistics, but I am guessing you have a plan."

"On a cruise! Think about it; bunch of partiers but confined to a ship, so they are most likely not going to be scary people, right?"

She hears G take a deep breath. "I swear I will never understand your logic. Why England and Spain? There are thousands of cruises from New York."

"Yes, but there is a good chance I might know someone on that cruise, and I prefer it to be a total stranger."

"Again, can't argue with that logic."

"You've had one-night stands. Why is it different if I want one?"

"It's not, and Claudia will keep an eye on you, so I am not worried about it."

"Will you just tell me if this is a good cruise line? I emailed you the one I want."

"Hang on, let me pull up my email. Good thing I don't have to be in court today—oh, wait. Yes, I do."

"Well then, you'll want to be snappy about this, won't you?"

"Boy, you are bossy today! Wait a sec, I'm pulling it up....Okay, my dear, this cruise line is a very good choice for you. Excellent reviews and an upscale clientele."

"Sweet! Thanks, G. I'm going to book it today. Hope I can get something in the next few weeks."

"That's what I am here for. Let me know what week you decide on. Catch ya later."

G hangs up the phone and begins to ponder the conversation he just had with Kate. He is not sure how he feels about all of this. She might need more of a chaperone than that sex-crazed Claudia. He checks his schedule for the next few weeks to see if he can get away for any amount of time. He also checks on flights to London.

TWO

A mere five days later, Kate and Claudia are packed and heading to the airport. Kate decides to spare no expense for her trip with Claudia, from first-class plane tickets to a five-star London hotel to the finest suites on the cruise itself. She is not usually an extravagant spender, but this seemed like the right time to splurge.

"You really know how to treat a girl!" Claudia tells her with an appreciative smile. Coming from Claudia, this is a huge compliment. She looks right at home in the first-class section as the flight attendant hands them two flutes of champagne.

"Well, there's no one else I'd rather go on a hunt for a one-night stand with!" Kate replies with a soft smile on her face. The man across the aisle overhears their conversation and makes a face, but the woman sitting next to him seems to approve and smiles at Kate and Claudia.

"Just promise me you'll sample the buffet before you decide to fall in love with someone," Claudia says, sounding somewhat concerned.

"Claudia, you know that's not the plan," Kate reassures her friend. "I had the love of my life, and there will never be another. I have accepted that. I am okay with that. I am only going because I want to have sex. Nothing more!"

Again, the man across the aisle seems annoyed by the direction of their conversation. Again, his wife seems just the opposite. In fact, she is extremely interested in their conversation, listening intently as the two friends talk.

"Kate, darling," Claudia begins, "I thought the same thing too after Antonio died, but I found love again. Many times!" She sips her champagne and adds, "Sweetie, it's been three years. For some people, that's enough; for others, it's not. You'll know when the time is right. All I'm saying is just don't close the door."

Kate gives Claudia her "I appreciate what you are saying, but my mind is made up" look, which Claudia brushes off, pressing the issue a bit further. "I'm sure you remember that feeling when you would meet Peter. You remember how you couldn't wait to see him and got all weak in the knees when you finally did, right? I just want you to know that it can happen again."

Kate takes a deep breath and says, "That's because we met in college, and that's what young lovers do. And we were supposed to grow old together and sit on our front porch in rocking chairs watching our grandchildren play, but now that's not going to happen. And you more than anyone know what I went through the last year before he died. I have zero interest in dealing with anything like that again..." Her voice trails off.

The flight attendant arrives with more champagne, softening the blow.

"I'm sorry, babes," Claudia says softly before reaching for her friend's hand.

"It's okay," Kate says with a shake of her head, as if to clear the sad thoughts away as well. "Besides, what I want doesn't exist anyway."

"Oh, and exactly what boxes have you checked off for your perfect man?"

"Well, first of all, he needs to be kind to animals," Kate explains, sipping her champagne.

"That's a given," Claudia nods.

"He needs to know how to dance, be spiritual, have similar taste in music, and be a Yankee fan—or at least not a Red Sox fan."

"That's very interesting...," Claudia says as though she's thinking of something.

"What?" Kate asks her friend.

"You pretty much want everything in a man that G is not!" Claudia laughs.

"Yeah, well, pretty much. You know I don't have feelings for him. And I know you don't particularly like him, but he always has my back, and he makes me laugh."

"He *is* easy on the eyes; I'll give him that," Claudia says. Then she adds, "Okay, Universe! You heard her order. Now get to work!"

They clink their champagne glasses, have a good laugh, and settle in to enjoy the rest of their flight.

While Claudia has her nose in a book, Kate turns to look out the window and thinks immediately of G. It is true that he has the exact opposite tastes for things from sports teams to music to even food. He cannot stand being around animals, and you won't catch him anywhere near a dance floor these days. Kate laughs to herself, remembering how G calls spirituality "mumbo jumbo stuff." She also fantasizes about him kissing her. Slowly undressing her. Running her hands across his chest. Wild sex on the balcony of his penthouse.

When they reach London, the two friends hail a taxi. On the way to their hotel, Kate gazes out the window at London's bustling streets and historic sights. She is absolutely amazed. Claudia grew up here, so for her this is a stroll down memory lane. Kate, however, is a London virgin. And for her, this is the ultimate way to start the new adventure she is hoping will be the missing ingredient to her becoming a world-famous author.

In Kate's eyes, London looks every bit like the pictures she had seen prior to their arrival. Quaint little streets, pubs on every corner, giant cathedrals, and so much history. Oh, the history! Westminster, Big Ben, and Buckingham Palace. She is thrilled to have Claudia as a tour guide. Kate is so busy taking in the sights that she doesn't notice the traffic is at a standstill. All too familiar with London gridlock, Claudia is easily agitated.

"This traffic is worse than New York!" she exclaims.

As Kate stares out the window of the now-still taxi, taking in all she can, Claudia reaches into Kate's bag, pulls out a cruise brochure, and unfolds it. "Uh, Kate, how much research did you do on this cruise?" she asks with a bemused expression.

With her nose still stuck to the window, Kate rattles off what she knows: "Well, the ship is brand new; they get raves for their food—in and out of London, stop in Spain for a beach resort area. They have ballroom dancing every night! That was a clincher for me; sorry, but there's lots to do."

"I see."

Sensing something is on her friend's mind, Kate hesitantly adds, "Why do you ask?"

"Well," Claudia drawls, "I was just noticing that all the people pictured in the photos are, um, well, grayish."

Unsure what Claudia means and seeking clarification, Kate blankly repeats the word, "Grayish?"

"Like, *old*," Claudia snorts, holding up the brochure like she was spreading out a fan. True enough, Kate notices that all the people pictured in the brochure do indeed appear grayish. Kate's excitement at being in London, starting her adventure, is quickly dashed, and her smile turns to a frown.

She should have known this wasn't meant to be! Why is she trying, yet again, to be something she isn't? This must be a sign from the universe that, despite her careful planning, other things are bound to happen to thwart those plans. Normally this is when Kate bails, be it finishing a novel, following through with plans outside her comfort zone, or the many times she let fear hold her back.

Claudia quickly senses Kate's disappointment and deftly steers the conversation to something more upbeat. "Hey, no sad faces! Look at the bright side. There won't be any competition!"

Kate knows she can rely on her friend. "I don't know what I would do without you. Actually, I know what I would do. I would turn right around and head back to New York."

The taxi driver, a good-looking young man, couldn't help but overhear the conversation, and enjoys what he has heard. Claudia notices him looking back at them in the rearview mirror.

"I don't mean to interrupt," he chimes, "but if you lovely ladies are looking for a good time tonight, Excalibur has it all. Six rooms playing all kinds of music, lots of people, and everyone dressed to impress."

"It sounds interesting!" Claudia answers.

At that, the driver hands her two passes over his shoulder. One has his name and number on it. "If you need a ride later," he says, turning to look Claudia over, "give me a call."

Kate stays quiet and listens to the two of them talk. She can listen to that British accent all day long! Just as traffic starts to pick up, Kate realizes they are in the theater district and notices a theater with "HAMILTON" on the marquee. "Claudia, look!"

Claudia is obsessed with anything Broadway. When she was younger, she camped out like a teenager at the stage door, hoping to get a glimpse of one of the actors or actresses. The only time Kate has ever seen Claudia speechless was when Nathan Lane came out after a night of *The Producers*. As he signed an autograph for her, he asked her something, and all she could manage was a squeak. *Hamilton* was her current favorite. Goodness knows what sound she would make if she ever got within ten feet of Lin-Manuel Miranda.

"Ah, my love!" Claudia sighs.

The driver notices and says, "I had him in this very taxi just a few days ago. Dropped him off at that theater."

"He's here? In London?" Claudia erupts, looking frantically around the cab, grabbing the door handle and sighing as though she would find Lin-Manuel Miranda there. Kate fears her friend might explode with excitement. Typically, Claudia is cool as a cucumber, but upon hearing how close she is to Lin-Manuel Miranda, she becomes a teenager gushing about her high school crush.

"You okay?" the driver asks.

Claudia is still in her Hamilton bubble, so Kate reassures the driver. "Yeah, she just has a thing for him."

As Claudia makes her way back to earth, she declares, "He is a genius! For real, though, you know he won the Pulitzer. Also, his music is brilliant. He's the only man who could get me to watch a Broadway play with rap and hip-hop in it and still love it. His *Hamilton* is superb and truly a work of genius. There's no other word for it."

"Let's try to get tickets tonight!" Kate says.

"You're sweet, but after seeing him in it, no other production would be the same. Besides," Claudia taps the Excalibur passes on Kate's leg, "we are going out tonight, my dear." Claudia's enthusiasm for the night has Kate a little worried.

Claudia is ready for a night on the town. As always, she's dressed like she stepped straight out of the pages of *Vogue*, not a single hair out place, primed to makes her presence known with beauty and confidence. She's also itching to get moving. Looking at her watch and sipping her drink, Claudia taps her foot. "Kate, darling," she calls, "will you shake a leg, please? I want to get there before it's too—" She stops in mid-sentence to admire her friend, who has just walked into the room. Kate is transformed, shedding her comfy travel outfit in favor of a sleek black dress that hugs her curves in all the right places. Its zip-up front is zipped down just enough to highlight Kate's ample bosom. Her long brown hair cascades in loose curls all around her face. Voluminous, long, and wavy, it looks perfect with her outfit.

"Wow, you look fantastic!" Claudia says after a moment of stunned silence.

"I do, don't I?" Kate smiles. "I'm so glad you convinced me to do yoga."

"It only took three years to convince you," Claudia quips.

"I know, it takes me a bit to try something new."

Claudia raises an eyebrow. "A bit?" She loves her friend and cherishes their friendship, but watching her retreat into her shell these past few years has been hard for Claudia. Kate has always been the constant, reliable one, but when she let her hair down, she could be funny, charming, and fun-loving. During her marriage and while raising Chelsea, she managed to keep the two Kates separate, but once Peter died, the fun-loving Kate seemed to disappear.

"Let's not keep London waiting!" Claudia's battle cry makes Kate smile.

"Oh, wait a sec," Kate pauses. "I promised G a selfie. Come here." The two ladies pose for the camera, making their most seductive come-hither looks.

"What is G up to these days?" Claudia asks, but Kate doesn't answer. She's busy sending the photo with the caption: "Here's a selfie before the drinking starts. Stay tuned for the drunk texts." The texting marathon with G has started and, like most times, should extend late into the night. G knows when Kate has had a glass or two of wine, as her texts get very flirty.

Remembering Claudia's question, Kate abruptly says, "Oh, he's G. He has a new flavor of the month, Alexandra. So he's not as chatty as when he's between lady friends. I talked to him the other day, though, long enough to upset the new one." She's proud of the fact, and not afraid to let out a little chuckle.

"He never married, huh?"

"Nope, and he certainly had plenty of chances. I don't think I could count how many girlfriends he's had."

"You ever like any of them?"

"Not a one!" Kate says defiantly as she struts toward the door.

"Interesting," Claudia murmurs to herself as she shuts the door behind her. Kate hears her and knows better than to protest. Claudia has been dead sure that Kate has been pining over G for years, no matter how much Kate denies it.

The two make their way to Excalibur, which turns out to be a theme park of a nightclub. Its massive stone facade gives it a castle-like appearance—if castles also boasted red carpets, velvet ropes, and long lines of revelers waiting to get in. For Kate, this is reminiscent of the few times G took her out to clubs in New York. Although he was the super-popular high school jock and she the nerdy, shy bookworm, there were several occasions—because his mom made him, she was sure—that he invited her along when he went out with his friends. Kate enjoyed a peek inside his world, but she knew she didn't fit in.

After a few outings, she began declining all further invites, and he didn't press her.

The passes the taxi driver gave Claudia are VIP access, so they waltz right past the long lines and are inside the club within thirty seconds. It's a huge place, and the overall vastness of the place is overwhelming to Kate. There are people everywhere, and they all look sophisticated and stylish.

Claudia fits right in. Kate, even in her curve-hugging dress, does not. She finds herself gravitating, as always, toward the corners of the room to ride out the night. Doubts start to cross her mind again, and she begins to think that this is all a huge mistake on her part. Any time she tries to be something she isn't, it ends in disaster.

"Hey, I see that face!" Claudia admonishes. "Stop thinking! Use tonight as a warm-up for the cruise. Flirt a little, dance a little, and for heaven's sake, relax!" She hands a drink to Kate, who promptly and without a word gulps it down. Then, another. "Whew! Let's mingle!" Claudia attempts to lead Kate through the crowd.

Kate feels her phone buzz, pulls aside, and sees a response from G: "Look out, London! Cougars on the loose!"

"Cougars?" Kate responds.

"You do know what a cougar is?"

"It's an animal, so what does that have to do with anything?"

"Cougars are older women who prey on young studs like me."

"You do remember you're older than me?"

"Only by twenty-three days!"

"We're at a club. Claudia is trying to get me in the swing for the cruise."

"Oh, yeah, the old people cruise. Did you see the Yankees lost? Ouch."

"Stop picking on my Yankees. How did you know it was an old people cruise?"

"I looked up the cruise line, remember?"

25

"And you didn't think to mention that to me?"

"I figured that was your speed."

Claudia returns to see Kate busy with her phone in hand. Noticing Kate's expression, she asks, "You okay?"

"*Ooh!* He just bugs the crap out of me sometimes."

"Who?"

"G."

"Interesting. Now put the phone down," Claudia chides, "and go mingle with people that are actually here." With that, she snatches Kate's phone and slides it in her purse. Then she shoos Kate into the middle of the dance floor.

As Claudia turns to head back to the bar, Kate decides she would be way more comfortable away from the crowd; she steers toward a less crowded area around the back of a staircase leading to the balcony. She surveys the crowd, realizing that she doesn't really want to be here. She looks down at her watch and figures she needs to last another hour before she can hassle Claudia to head back to the hotel. When she picks her head up again, she notices a young man walking across the floor toward the stairs. He looks around thirty years old. He is tall, slender, and has perfect hair. He moves across the floor with a confident stride, but there is something about him that makes Kate think he has something on his mind. Every woman that he walks past tries to catch his attention, but he wants no part. He is focused on getting to the staircase without making eye contact with anyone. Her curiosity thoroughly piqued, she wonders where he is going. She decides to follow him.

That should keep me busy for a while, Kate thinks as she begins her subtle pursuit. *And I can report back to Claudia that I was mingling.*

She ascends the staircase that leads up to the balcony, all the while keeping her eye on her mystery man. Once he reaches the top, he turns left and walks quickly down a long hallway. He then enters a room at the end. Kate scurries along, making sure not to lose sight of her target. For some unexplainable reason, she is very interested in where he is going. The room has two large doors that swing in and out. Every time someone enters or leaves the room, she hears music pulsing through the breach. There is a familiar vibe to the music. She slowly pushes open one of the doors and, to her surprise, finds a decent-sized crowd dancing to one of her favorite songs. Her mystery man is nowhere to be seen, but a nice-looking man standing next to her leans in and asks, "Don't you just love this music? This room has the best music in all of Excalibur."

"Yes, my favorite," Kate replies. She's not interested, but at least now she can truthfully report back to Claudia that she talked to someone tonight.

"Would you like to dance?" he asks her abruptly.

Kate hesitates for a second, but the drinks she downed are now providing some liquid encouragement. So she decides, what the heck!

"Yes, I would!"

The man holds out his hand and walks Kate to the dance floor. Once there, he immediately puts his arms around her and starts dancing way too close for Kate's comfort. This is not what she expected, and she is feeling rather uncomfortable. She pushes him back just enough to politely indicate that she does not want to be held so closely or tightly. Unfortunately, the man doesn't take the hint, and in fact pulls her back in rather forcefully.

Kate struggles to step back. That's when her mystery man comes out of nowhere. He grabs the guy and says something to him that Kate can't make out. Then, just like that, the offending party walks away.

"Are you okay?" the mystery man asks, looking at Kate right in the eyes with a look that makes her want to melt.

"Yes, I think so," she slowly manages to say. "It's been quite a while since I went dancing, but that was a little too intense for me. Thank you for your help."

"You are welcome. Dancing should not be like that."

Kate detects an accent, but it's not British.

"This music is so good. It brings back a lot of memories," Kate says in an attempt to keep the conversation going.

"I am glad you like it. I am the DJ; I am—"

Kate interrupts him as soon as she hears the opening of the next song. "Oh, my gosh! I love this song! I haven't heard it in years!"

"Come then," he says. "Let us dance to it the proper way." His accent makes her heart flutter.

Without hesitation or the slightest care how the previous dance went, Kate accepts his invitation. Immediately, he spins her around and starts dancing hustle, a dance she's familiar with from all the time she and Peter spent taking dance lessons at a local ballroom studio.

Her head begins to spin from the rush of excitement. To be dancing again! To one of her favorite songs! With a very good-looking younger man! Who has the dreamiest accent and even dreamier eyes! A man who certainly knows how to dance!

The two dance for what feels like an eternity. They dance together in sync. He is commanding the dance floor, and Kate is so engulfed in the dance that she is overjoyed and overwhelmed by it all. The entire time, the two of them keep staring at each other, never once breaking eye contact.

He spins her out and back in. Then he makes a move she has never seen before. Still, she follows because he's a masterful lead. He smiles at her, and she feels his eyes and smile touch her soul. The song morphs into another song, and they don't miss a beat. The two of them keep on dancing.

With the way he showers her with attention, Kate feels like a princess. She feels like she's on cloud nine. The song slows down; the masterful mystery man brings Kate in then sends her back into a long slow dip. As she comes back up, the two of them are finally face-to-face, staring right into each other's eyes.

28

Almost at the same time, they both move in closer, their lips touching ever so gently. When their lips finally part, Kate and her mystery man are still looking at each other. They smile and then lean into one another. Right there, in the middle of the dance floor, they share a passionate kiss. They begin to move while still locked in their embrace. The door to the DJ booth bursts open, and they both tumble in.

His hands are around her waist, and slowly they begin to explore. First they move up to her shoulders; then they begin to glide down, sliding along the curve of her breasts. They move toward her hips and then to her ass. The mystery man lifts Kate onto the back table attached to the wall. Kate runs her hands all over his chest and shoulders. She reaches one hand around to his ass. She can feel just how excited he is when he leans in to kiss her again.

He starts to unbutton his jeans and slowly unzips the front of her dress. Distracted by something, he realizes that the music has stopped. He looks out of the DJ booth to see everyone standing in confusion, looking around. They can't see inside the booth, but they're starting to make noise to get the music back on.

"*Merda!*" he murmurs. Kate knows enough street Italian from being around G to know that her mystery man isn't very happy.

"Do not go anywhere," he tells Kate with a kiss. He runs to the other side of the booth and starts punching keys on his laptop. As he gets to the bottom of the issue, Kate slowly drifts back to reality. She looks at her state of undress and the man across the room, with whom she was just about to have sex.

At once, her ecstasy turns into despair. She had been feeling excitement and desire, but it was now replaced with guilt and awkwardness. She quickly jumps off the table and bolts for the door. She hurries outside without saying another word to the mystery man.

The DJ apologizes to the crowd. He turns back to the woman he was about to ravish, teasing aloud, "Now, where were we?" But the room is empty, the door just closing behind the woman who has left. He buttons his pants and takes off into the crowd.

Kate rushes down the stairs, weaving through the thick crowd with desperation. *Oh, please be where I left you, Claudia,* she thinks as she crosses the large main room. She finds her friend at the bar.

"Claudia, we need to go. *Now!*" She grabs her friend's hand and leads her to the exit.

"Hey, what's up?" Claudia asks as she tugs on Kate's arm.

Kate turns to answer but sees her mystery man at the top of the stairs, scanning the crowd for her. Quickly she explains, "I did something I shouldn't have, and I really want to not be here, so can we go please?"

Outside, Kate frantically tries to wave down a taxi, to no avail. Claudia steps in front of her and says, "Here, allow me." With one whistle and the tip of her hand, a taxi instantly appears in front of them. Kate wastes no time getting in the taxi and telling the driver the name of the hotel.

"Okay, so what is going on? And why is your dress unzipped?" Claudia's voice is laced with concern for her friend.

Kate, still breathless from all that has happened, starts to relay the events of the past hour. "I followed this really good-looking guy upstairs, and there was this room that was playing the really good dance music, you know, the stuff I really like. Then this creepy guy— well I didn't know he was creepy at the time—asked me to dance."

Kate takes a long breath, and Claudia asks, "Did he hurt you?"

"He just wouldn't let me go!"

"Oh, my gosh!"

"I know!" Kate continues. "So, I pushed him away, and he kept trying to dance with me, and that's when the really good-looking guy I followed jumped in and told the stranger to take a hike. He asked me if I was okay, and I said it'd been so long since I'd been dancing... and I didn't think I liked how people dance these days...and I really liked the music. He said he was the DJ and then asked me to dance the proper way."

Kate takes a deep breath, but when she starts talking again, her tone has changed from breathless and alarmed to controlled and wanting. "And he was such an amazing dancer; he dipped me—you know how I love dips—and when I came up, his face was like right here." She holds her hand up to her face. "And I don't know how it happened, but we kissed!"

Claudia, shocked to hear this from Kate, asks, "*You* kissed *him?*"

"*Yes!* Or he kissed me. I really don't know how it started."

"Way to go, sexy!"

"Wait, there's more. So at first, I am, like, whoa, what did I just do? But he smiled at me, and I just melted again, and we kissed again, and the next thing you know, we're in his DJ booth. I honestly don't even remember walking there, but we were kissing, and our hands were all over each other, and he lifted me up onto this table and started to unbutton his pants."

Kate pauses. Claudia notices that the taxi driver is paying more attention to Kate than the road. She signals him to stop. She pays him, and they get out of the car.

"Okay," Claudia says excitedly. "Now take a breath and slow down. This is getting good!"

"Then the music stopped, and he said, 'You don't go anywhere,' and went to fix it. And that's when I started to think. I got scared. I bolted and then came to find you."

Kate exhales. Claudia starts laughing.

"And just what part of all this is funny?" Kate asks, not amused.

"Oh, babes, it's not. I mean, it is. I'm just happy for you that you felt that feeling again—even if you left him hanging high and dry, probably with a huge hard-on!"

Kate finally relaxes. "I guess. I don't know. That kiss was so nice, and he was such a good dancer."

Now that the excitement has worn off, she looks sad.

"What's wrong?" Claudia asks.

"I'm such a dope! That would have been perfect; I should have stayed. I really don't know why I felt the need to leave."

"Because it's been a long time since you've been with anyone, so I guess you felt nervous. It took me a long time to get back in the saddle, so to speak."

"Well, this is exactly why I wanted to be as far away from home as possible. Could you imagine if this happened at home? I would be mortified!" Kate exclaims. "I wouldn't be able to go out for months!"

Claudia hugs her friend, and they start to walk the few remaining blocks to their hotel. "Kate, dear, you think everything is like it is in the movies. The odds of running into him again are like a gazillion to one. And I'm sure you definitely don't have to worry about running into him on the old people cruise, so just relax."

Back at the hotel, Kate settles into her bed with a smile on her face. She closes her eyes and imagines dancing with her mystery DJ.

She is startled back to reality by the *ding* of a text message.

"Where are the drunk texts?" It's G.

"None coming. I'm back at the hotel." Kate is too tired to think of a zippy comeback.

"Why so early? I thought you'd be a barfly for the night."

"Well, you'd be proud of me. I wasn't shy, that's for sure."

G scoffs, assuming Kate kept her back to the wall all night and is just trying to sound tough. "Okay, missy, what did you do?"

"I was dancing with a very cute and much younger guy, and all of a sudden we kissed."

After a minute, which is unusual for G, he responds, "You did what?"

"We kissed, then we kissed some more. A lot more."

Kate sees the "..." in the chat bubble, meaning G is typing. Then it disappears, then reappears, then disappears again.

"Don't tell me the great attorney is at a loss for words," she quips.

"No," comes the reply, "but you, evidently, are at a loss for morals."

Kate is starting to get annoyed by G's hypocrisy. "Funny, a lecture from the king of one-night stands. You know I needed to add steam to my book, so I'm trying. That's all that happened, though. I got scared and left."

"Just don't bring home an old dog or any diseases."

Kate is too angry at this point, so she thinks about what to say.

She ends up typing, "I've had enough excitement for the night."

That's all she cares to say. She knows he'll follow up with something funny like he always does, then they'll have a text fest and be laughing. She waits a few minutes for him to write back; when he doesn't, she lays down her phone, not expecting the conversation to end just like that. She tries to think of something snarky to say, but now really tired, she turns out the light and falls asleep quickly. She dreams about kissing her mystery man. When they pull away from each other, the man morphs into G. Instantly, she wakes up. Feeling a bit startled, she shakes her head and decides to go back to sleep.

Thousands of miles away, it is early evening in New York. G stares at Kate's picture on his phone.

"What are you doing, Kate?" he wonders aloud.

Alexandra walks in and sees the scowl on G's face. "Hey, babe, you okay? You look pissed."

G quickly puts his phone away. He certainly doesn't need Alexandra to see that he had been staring at Kate's picture. "Oh, uh, no, I'm fine. Just a client being...ah, never mind. No big deal."

Alexandra walks over to G and sits down on his lap. She faces him and gives him a long passionate kiss. Then she wraps her arms around him. Alexandra smiles. She is happy. But G certainly is not.

THREE

Kate wakes up the next morning with a smile on her face, remembering how it felt to kiss her mystery man. The memory is pleasant and soothing, but also like fire spreading through her veins. She smiles wider as she remembers the events of last night in more detail: his body pressed to hers, the feel of his soft lips on her own. The memory brings along a tingling feeling as she touches her lips with her fingertips.

That feeling fades, though, when she realizes that she left before anything else happened. An opportunity for something more skittered away due to a moment of indecision and hesitation. Why was that? She thinks for sure she had the perfect opportunity to experience some steamy sex, which is what she thought she wanted. And yet, she ran.

The thought of the fateful encounter and the kiss-and-run incident dredges up deeply buried thoughts and misgivings about her entire dilemma. Was it a mistake to come on this trip? Would the cruise experience prove any better? Maybe Claudia was right. It had been a long time since she was with someone, and a DJ booth in a club may be too far out there for her. Maybe the cruise will have a different vibe? Or maybe she needs to turn off her mind and just turn on the pleasure receptor, the part of her that has always wanted an adventure. But still she wishes others would have the same level of confidence in her that she sometimes wished for herself. It makes her mad that G thought the senior citizen cruise was more her speed. She hates it when he's right, and she would never let him know he was.

Arriving at the cruise dock, Kate is once again excited about the trip. Although she has a fear of the water, which dates back to her childhood, somehow this cruise ship doesn't paralyze her with fear. It's a good omen, one she welcomes with open arms. The reputation of the cruise line precedes the massive boat she is about to board. The ship itself offers much to tantalize all the guests' senses: opulent and tasteful decor, world-class service, decadent food made from the freshest ingredients, and of course, ballroom dancing every day and night. Kate misses dancing, but after Peter passed away, the thought of dancing did not appeal to her as much as it had in the past. She hopes this trip is a sign that she is ready to return to it.

She is also happy to have Claudia along with her. Claudia is a good friend. When her husband died, she threw herself into her career and raising her daughters. Unlike Kate, she had come into the marriage with a world of life experience, so once she decided she was ready to move on, move on she did—and with gusto. In short, Claudia is a perfect example of living the life you are in, relishing every moment. It's an attractive quality, one that Kate hopes to emulate and embrace one day, for she is always living in the past or waiting for the future to happen. Kate can learn a lot from her friend.

Claudia strolls past the other older guests, noticing most have gray hair. She glances at Kate with a smirk and rolls her eyes, but Kate knows her friend will make the most of the voyage. Once they step onto the deck, Claudia's eyes open wide and she smiles from ear to ear. Waiting to welcome the passengers is a line of ten crew members, one woman and nine men—each more handsome than the one before. "Now we're talking!" Claudia exclaims, a sparkle in her eyes.

"See, things are looking up! I'll have my shipboard you-know-what, you can have your fun, I'll finish my book, it will become a bestseller, they'll make a movie out of it, and you will be my date for the Oscars! I have four and a half days," Kate announces.

"And five nights," Claudia adds.

"And five nights to make that happen." Suddenly, Kate is feeling a lot more optimistic. Now is the time to come out of her shell and live in the moment, she tells herself.

At the obligatory lifeboat drill, Kate looks around and notices that most of the passengers seem to be couples, although there definitely are some single gentlemen that have noticed her and Claudia. They seem very sophisticated and very attractive. Her odds of having a fling are looking better. The sail-away party is not a crazy party like some other cruise lines, but instead a refined gathering with a string quartet and champagne. Kate notices the staff is much younger than the clientele and includes many handsome men. Kate follows Claudia's lead, chatting and flirting with mostly everyone she encounters. After a delightful dinner, they tour the ship before unpacking and calling it a night.

The morning sun glistens off the water and shines on Kate at the exact angle to wake her up. She slept with the balcony door open slightly to allow the sounds of the ocean to help her drift off to sleep. She stretches, feeling wonderfully rested and alive, raring to begin the new day. Slowly her mind drifts off to her mystery man. She thinks of the first kiss shared between them and how she tucked her tail between her legs and ran. However, she no longer cringes at what had happened. Everything happens for a reason, she reminds herself, even the turn her life has taken. She is now thankful to be on this senior citizen cruise.

Noticing the time, she checks one of the many brochures she picked up as they were strolling around last night. What she reads further confirms what she guessed soon after boarding the ship. All the activities are geared toward an older crowd, but the ballroom dancing schedule makes its way to the top of the pile. The brochure reads: "BALLROOM DANCING GROUP CLASS 11 A.M. JOIN WORLD-RENOWNED BALLROOM DANCER NIKOLAI PETROV FOR WALTZ IN THE MAIN BALLROOM."

The instructor's name doesn't ring a bell in Kate's head, but she decides to sign up for the class anyway. "Now that sounds like fun!" Kate jumps out of bed, a spring in her step as she heads to the closet and takes out her clothes for the day. She takes a little longer than normal to dress, and now she is ready to greet the day.

Wondering if Claudia is awake, she decides to check on her friend. Claudia's cabin is right next to hers. She knocks then calls through the door, "Hey it's me. Wanna go to a group class at eleven?"

A muffled groan comes from behind the door, which can only be from Claudia.

"I'll take that as a yes," Kate laughs. "I'm going to get breakfast."

Another groan.

"Okay, see you soon," Kate snickers before leaving. She knows her friend, so the best course of action right now is to go on with her plans until Claudia catches up. Besides, she's hungry, and breakfast awaits. Claudia can join any time after waking up.

The walk to the upper-deck dining room is short, but she still must take a flight of stairs. Kate's breath is taken away at first sight of the room. The dining hall features huge floor-to-ceiling windows and a beautiful view of the coastline. Most of the tables are filled with couples or groups of friends, so Kate asks for a small table by the window. She checks her phone out of habit. No signal. Just as well, she thinks. The more she can leave behind her, the better.

With her breakfast order placed, Kate dips into her bag and pulls out a notebook. Written across the cover, in fancy handwriting, are the words "Sleep Naked." She sighs and opens the notebook to the latest entry. This is one reason she wanted to come on the trip; "Sleep Naked" is Kate's attempt at writing steamy adult fiction. Inside is a collection of short, easy-to-read stories for adult women. She wants to write something more than romance, but not quite erotica. She wants something spicy, but not porn level. Sometimes she thinks G might be right: Maybe she is writing what she knows, and that's why it's not steamy.

"Okay, Universe," she scrunches her eyes in concentration, as if to will the words to her brain. "Give me some inspiration!" She opens her eyes, still staring at a blank page, then turns to the window. Soon a server comes to her table, bearing a plate of all her favorite breakfast items. He also delivers a cup of strong coffee, followed by the entire coffeepot. She closes the notebook to give attention to the hot breakfast, inhaling the aroma of the coffee as she smiles at the good food she is about to enjoy.

The shuffling of the chair across from her, followed by Claudia sitting down, distracts Kate momentarily. She looks up and sees Claudia's grumpy expression at having to wake up early. Judging from the scowl on her face, she is not a morning person. Kate smiles at her, nonetheless.

"Morning, sunshine!" Kate's friendly greeting is met with a look that makes her laugh even more. "Coffee?" She knows the answer before Claudia manages a nod and pushes the coffeepot in front of her friend.

"I ordered you some breakfast."

"Ah, bless you," her friend says, although Kate is not sure if Claudia is talking to her or to her coffee.

"Sleep okay?"

"Yes," Claudia answers, "but not enough. I will take a nap later. So, what is this group class about?"

"I wasn't sure if you heard me. Anyway, Nikolai Petrov is a famous ballroom dancer, or so it says in this brochure. He is teaching a waltz class this morning, and I signed us both up. Isn't that lovely?" Kate's sarcasm is not lost on her friend.

"Oh, yes, you know how much I love a good waltz," Claudia responds with corresponding irony.

"You can suffer through for an hour."

"I'm glad to see you aren't worried your mystery DJ is lurking around the corner."

Kate surveys the guests in the dining room. She and Claudia, forty-seven and forty-eight, respectively, are clearly the youngest passengers. "Yes, safe to say I don't have to worry about that."

The rest of the meal is spent talking about nothing and everything and laughing at past events that centered on the mystery man she had met.

—

The ship's ballroom is exquisite. Crystal chandeliers, mauve and gold accents, and a beautiful, spacious wood floor. They enter the majestic room, and her eyes widen. As she walks beside Claudia toward the dance floor, Kate gets that feeling deep down, that excited feeling... and, oh, how she has missed that! Even the chairs are tufted velvet. She sits down to put her dance shoes on, and she sighs.

"Earth to Kate! Are you in there?" Claudia interrupts.

"Oh, sorry, just reminiscing. I'm feeling good about this. Wow, my shoes literally have dust on them." Kate blows on them, and a cloud of the stuff floats to the floor.

"One of a few things you need to have dusted off," Claudia observes with a chuckle.

Kate and Claudia make their way onto the dance floor and find a spot equally in the mix but also on the fringe of the group. Claudia is taking cues from Kate and is careful to not push her to do more than she thinks Kate can handle. As they wait, Kate fills Claudia in on Nikolai Petrov's background, which she found out thanks to a quick stop before breakfast to the ship's library and its computer terminals.

"So, Nikolai is a Russian ballroom dancer, now in his early forties; he had a long career in dancing and won many titles. When he retired from dancing, he and his partner, whom he married, opened a chain of studios in Russia. In a nasty divorce, he left the studios behind for a life at sea, still doing what he loves to do."

"Wow! Talk about the epic highs and lows of a Russian ballroom dancer. Could totally be a title for a book."

"Oh, and he loves Bach."

"Good to know. You weren't checking to make sure he wasn't your mystery DJ, were you?"

Kate smiles. A look of embarrassed guilt crosses her face, quickly replaced by a mischievous glance. She was caught! "Well, maybe the thought did cross my mind."

"Oh, Kate! You are so obvious!" Claudia laughs at Kate's antics, then quickly directs her eyes at a newcomer.

"Who is *that*?"

"I think he is our instructor."

Nikolai emerges from the side and walks—no, *strides*—toward the middle of the room. He's a very handsome man, almost six feet tall and definitely in good shape. His sandy blond hair is ruffled about his face, and he has the most distinguished features.

And, it turns out, an accent!

"Ladies and gentlemen," he announces, "welcome to the *Princess of the Seas*. Today's class was supposed to be a waltz, but there is a slight change if you don't mind. It's a very good change, I think you will agree with me. A very good friend of mine has joined me at the last minute on the voyage, and he just happens to be a former two-time ten dance champion. I had to ask nicely, but he was happy to step in to teach today's class."

A strange feeling creeps over Kate. She looks at Claudia with a worried look. Claudia knows how her friend thinks and tries to reassure her: "There is no way. Relax! Not the movies, remember."

Kate peers around her to get a look at the guest teacher. Nikolai walks to the middle of the floor and raises his voice slightly as if introducing a celebrity guest on a late-night talk show.

"Ladies and gentlemen, please welcome my good friend, Luca Bell'Angelo!"

The group of people in the room give him a nice round of applause. Out steps a very handsome man, who confidently, almost arrogantly, walks across the floor to join his friend. Claudia watches the color drain from Kate's face.

"Is that him?" she whispers. "Don't tell me that's your mystery DJ!"

Kate's eyes grow wide. She nods and retreats to hide behind Claudia.

Realizing it's her job to help Kate hold it together, Claudia tries to reassure her friend.

"You really think he will recognize you? It was dark, and you look totally different than you did that night."

Any doubt Kate has that she will go unrecognized disappears with Nikolai's next words: "Luca is a real-life hero, ladies and gentlemen. The other night, he was at a club in London, where he came to the rescue of a lovely young lady who was being harassed by an awful man."

A round of *oohs* and *aahs* erupt from the crowd, followed by appreciative glances directed at Luca, who is beaming at the applause and attention.

"Oh, it was nothing!" he shrugs with fake modesty. "I did not even get her name, but I hope she is okay." He looks squarely at Kate. "Wherever she may be."

There is a brief pause.

"Now, let us dance!" he snaps. With a click of a remote, the song "Last Night a DJ Saved My Life" begins blaring from the speakers. Everyone chuckles at the choice, but not Kate.

"I think he knows," she whispers to Claudia.

"Well, rise above it. Act like it was no big deal. I can't imagine he'll call you out in front of this crowd."

"Okay, everyone! I am going to show you the whole sequence, then we will break it down. So, I need someone to help me." Luca rubs his hands together and scans the crowd. His gaze passes over the group of people and finally stops on Kate. "Miss? Please, would you come to help me demonstrate?"

Luca is locked on Kate, who is now flustered and looking anywhere but in his direction. The woman next to her taps her on the shoulder. "Honey, he's talking to you."

Kate looks helplessly at her friend. Claudia shrugs her shoulders and gives her the "I'm sorry but get out there" look before pushing Kate forward. With the little nudge of encouragement from Claudia, Kate slowly walks toward the middle of the room and stops a few feet short of Luca.

"You can come closer, *si*," he says coyly. "I do not bite."

Kate recalls his dreamy voice from the other night.

"You do nibble, though," she stammers in an attempt to lighten the mood a little. Luca smiles, the kind of smile that says, "Yes, I remember, and I enjoyed every minute of it." He reaches for her hand.

"And what is your name?"

"Kate."

"Everyone, say hello to Kate."

The crowd obliges with a hearty, "Hello, Kate!"

"Hello, Kate," Luca whispers, fascinated at hearing her name. After all, this is the first time he has. Still whispering in her ear, he gives her goosebumps as he says, "Follow along like you did the other night. Stay for the whole thing this time."

Suddenly, the air around them charges with electricity, and Kate's senses hone straight toward the man, his every movement, his voice, and the feel of his strong, warm hand against her own. He winks at her, which almost puts her over the edge.

Forcing herself not to think too much about the chills shooting through her entire body, Kate turns to Claudia and mouths, *"Help me!"* But Claudia knows better. She wants to let this play out. She demonstrates a proper posture and a smile, hoping Kate will follow this silent order. Much to her delight, she does.

On the other hand, Kate doesn't know what to do or say to the man who has turned her life upside down just by appearing on the same cruise as her, not to mention teaching the same class she signed up for. Desperately wanting to break the ice, Kate mutters, "Interesting song choice."

"I thought so. Are you ready?"

"As ready as I'll ever be."

The music starts. Luca does some basic hustle steps, then adds a few spins and ends with a slow dip. The entire crowd feels the sexual energy between Luca and Kate as he slowly brings her up until they are face-to-face. Kate blushes.

"Everyone ready to try, yes?" The women in the class are clearly excited, but most of the men look a little nervous. "I will to break it down for you. Take a partner." Luca holds on to Kate's hand as she starts to back up. "Not you. You are mine for the next forty-five minutes."

"I can explain about the other night."

"*Si*, yes, you will, but right now, you help me to demonstrate." Kate purses her lips; she's about to say something snarky but holds the words back. Instead, she focuses on the class and the movements of the man beside her, the man whose very existence seems to ignite a fire within her body. She slowly begins to relax and even enjoy being the center of attention, which is unusual for her. But when you have a handsome, younger man dancing with you, it's easy to blur your surroundings.

The dance continues as Luca guides Kate through the steps, stopping every few minutes to point things out to the class. This surprises Kate, as most professionals never want to give students the time of day. Luca is really being nice, patient, and thorough. He shows off when he has the chance and does a little something extra or holds her close. He has piqued the interest of the dancers in the group.

"How do you do those extra turns?" one man asks, looking perplexed. Luca does two with Kate and explains the proper technique, so the follower knows what is expected.

Luca asks Kate, "Can you do more than two turns?"

"Yes, my record is seven, but you'll have to hold on to me at the end to make sure I don't fall over."

"I can be okay with that," he assures in his imperfect English. "I will to make sure you do not fall over." His cute little grin makes her smile back at him.

Luca twirls Kate seven times at the perfect point of the song, then he stops her, pulls her leg slowly up his side, and lowers her back into a long dip. The crowd applauds.

"Now remember, when you want her to stop, you have to send her a signal, and that is easily done by placing your palm on her back, like this." He demonstrates the move, his hand resting on her back maybe a little longer than necessary. Then he continues, "Okay, adventurers, who is going to try a few turns."

Luca seems to enjoy watching everyone try. Claudia's partner must have missed the part about stopping; he put his hand up too late and it landed right on her boob. However, being the good sport Claudia is, and knowing it was an accident, she just laughs it off.

Halfway through the class, Luca sees everyone is picking it up. "Okay, now, let me show the leaders how to do a proper dip. Very important for all you followers to do your part and push your hips up, or—"

Just then, Claudia and her partner crash to the floor.

"That." Luca says with a smile. "You two okay?"

"Yeah," Claudia grumbles as she gets up, rubbing her backside. "Just peachy."

Looking at the clock, Luca announces, "We have just only ten minutes left. Everyone line up: followers here, leaders here. Practice the syncopation once then switch. Leaders move to left. I will come around to help if needed."

He then turns to Kate, still holding her hand in a gentle but firm grip. "Is it safe to let you go for a few minutes?" he asks with a twinkle in his eye.

"I can't swim, so I'll be here," she answers, walking over to the followers' line. Within seconds, she is surrounded by gentlemen eager to dance with her. *Hmm, this is interesting,* she thinks, amazed at the fact that she is enjoying the attention when normally she would have bolted—or avoided the entire situation in the first place.

After a few minutes, the class officially ends. Nikolai comes out to the center of the floor again.

"Thanks to Luca and Kate for a great class! Any questions?"

"When is the next class?!" one woman asks. Several of the ladies nod in agreement.

"Tomorrow morning, rumba at eleven," Nikolai says. "But tonight, there's a dance party right here starting at eight o'clock. Hope to see everyone. You can all practice what you learned today. And remember, ladies, proper dance etiquette is to accept all dances."

The group starts to disperse. Kate stands rooted to her spot until Claudia approaches from behind to say, "So that is the mystery man, huh? I approve. Not sure I would have bolted."

"Yeah, pretty dumb move, I know. At least he was pretty cool about it. I thought it was going to get ugly for a minute there."

46

Just as the words leave her mouth, Luca walks over, smiles at Claudia, introduces himself, and kisses the back of her hand. Claudia blushes. Kate doesn't ever remember seeing Claudia blush. This Luca is a real charmer.

Claudia reads the situation and quickly picks up her things to excuse herself. "See you at lunch, Kate." She gives her friend a quick kiss on the cheek, making sure to sneak a cute little cat sound in Kate's ear.

"Thanks for coming," Kate says as Claudia walks away. "Sorry about the boob grab and getting dropped." In typical fashion, Claudia shrugs it off and signals no big deal with a wave. Luca and Kate are now alone in the ballroom.

Luca's mood changes the minute Claudia is outside of the ballroom.

Again, the air around them sizzles with electricity as Luca says in a low tone, "Okay, now is your chance to explain and apologize."

"Wait, what? Apologize? For what?"

"For getting me all hot...and then sneaking out when I look away for a second, especially after I saved your ass from that creep."

"First of all, I had every right to walk away, and I should have said something, but I didn't, so for *that* I apologize."

"You do not know what you walked away from. Women would kill to be with me."

"Holy cow! You are an arrogant son of..." Kate trails off. "How does your big head fit through the doorway?"

"If you had stayed around long enough, you would have found out." Luca looks down at his crotch.

"Oh, my gosh! How full of yourself! You might be a great dancer, but your people skills need some work."

"My people skills work just fine. You should work on yours."

"Seriously, what are you? Like ten?"

"That's about right." He smirks at Kate, who is confused for a moment before slowly registering the double entendre. She feels her face flush and struggles to maintain her composure at the crude words leaving the man's sexy but arrogant mouth. Luca is talking about size even though Kate means age. He smiles at her and raises his eyebrows.

Kate doesn't know what to say. "Wow, okay. I think I'll just go." She starts to pick up her things, then pauses and says, "For a minute I thought I regretted leaving the other night, but now I am sure I made the right decision. *This* time you can watch me walk away." Kate heads for the door and doesn't turn around.

Luca is not sure what to say. He's confused. Ladies don't walk away from him. The best he can do is convince himself because, the truth is, Kate has rattled him. "There will be a hundred others lined up," he yells in her direction.

Kate doesn't take kindly to his comment. "As long as you're happy," she hisses as she slams the door behind her.

Luca sits down in a chair, a peculiar expression on his face. He lets out a sigh and says, "Women!"

Kate walks to the dining room and heads to the same table, where she finds Claudia. She plops down and exhales, "Hmph! What a jerk!"

"I listened outside the door for a few minutes," Claudia says. "Well, there you go. It's over now. You can have a good time and take care of what you came to do."

Kate was clearly not letting it go. "I cannot get over how full of himself he is."

"Don't let him ruin your trip. He's an egomaniac. Forget about him."

"You're right! I'm not giving that jerk another thought. Let's eat, and then I'm going to the gym to punch something."

Even though she says it, she doesn't believe she can let it go. Maybe she doesn't want to. Luca stirred up something in her, again, that she has not felt in a long time. Whatever it is, it feels good, and she wants more.

FOUR

If Kate's good at one thing, it is pushing things to the back of her mind and moving on as if events don't bother her in the slightest. She decides to try the same strategy with Luca and the recent events that have transpired between them. It's unfortunate that the mysterious man of that wonderful night just *had* to be aboard the ship, a friend of the resident dance instructor, but such a twist in events can—and must—be overlooked.

Kate and Claudia are in the dining room, having just finished a scrumptious dinner. Kate certainly has her focus back, and the events of the disastrous morning seem to be a distant memory now.

"What a great dinner!" she exclaims. "Did I not tell you how good the food was going to be? Simply marvelous! The beef Wellington! Yum!"

"Yes, darling," Claudia says. "I remember you gushing on and on about the three-course dinners. I personally liked the scallops better, though. So decadent."

Claudia lounges back on the chair, a satisfied look on her face. Silence reigns at the table for a few moments as Kate sips from her wine glass and looks around the dining hall. The patrons sitting at the other tables are immersed in laughter and chatter. Kate looks at Claudia, who's still basking in the afterglow of the good meal.

"I was thinking, why don't we go to the lounge from here? I heard there is a great piano player who can play any tune."

"Sure, but I will catch up with you in about an hour. I am going to meet Paolo on the top deck for some stargazing."

"Paolo? Who's Paolo?"

"He was one of the officers we met on the way in. Don't you remember? Of course you don't. You had your eyes everywhere but on the men. Anyway, he's going to teach me about navigating under the stars."

Kate detects a gleam in Claudia's eye as she empties her wine glass and licks her lips one last time. She knows what that means in Claudia's world, and she smirks as she teases her best friend: "Well, have fun. I'd say don't do anything I wouldn't do, but there is no danger of that. I'll see what I can stir up myself, if ya know what I mean."

"Yes, I do, and I hope you find what you're looking for. Stay away from the ballroom if a certain someone is there."

"Yes, Mother."

Even though she rolls her eyes, Kate knows Claudia is right. Luckily Luca's not the only man on the ship. There seems to be an ample supply of men on this cruise, so she just needs to stay focused. Claudia rises from her seat and gives Kate a kiss on the cheek before walking out of the dining room.

After Claudia leaves, Kate decides to change into something a little sexier. After all, she has brought a suitcase full of Claudia's sexy clothes, whether to attract men or to feel nice herself. She makes her way to the cabin and rummages through her closet for the perfect attire. Finally, she picks a bronze one-shoulder dress, short and tight in all the right places. She has long legs and figures sitting at the piano is a good way to show them off.

Let the games begin, she tells herself before striding gracefully to the lounge, amused at how she feels so different in just a few days.

———

The lounge has a very old-world library feel to it. The bar, which runs down the whole right side of the room, is made of a rich, dark wood, with mirrors behind the shelves and deep green leather bar stools. A large piano is nestled in a little alcove on the left, surrounded by cushy swivel chairs. In the middle of the room is a small dance floor, unoccupied at the moment.

The lounge is not crowded at all. Kate figures that everyone must still be at dinner—or at the dance party. She would have gone but did not want to run the risk of another encounter with Luca. She doesn't do well with confrontation. In fact, she is surprised she handled the morning as well as she did. Yes, the lounge is a safe place, and Claudia will be along soon.

Kate surveys the room and decides to sit down at the first stool near the piano. The gentleman playing is a good-looking man in his fifties, or so she guessed. With a tinge of gray set against his tan face, he looks like he could be on an album cover. Kate figures she'll flirt a little and see how that goes.

"Hi."

"Well, hello there, my first customer," the man says warmly. "Take a seat, young lady. I'm Sam. Yes, Sam, the piano player. Original, I know. What's your name? Where are you from? And why are you by yourself?"

Sam is as smooth as they come. He plays the piano well and has a talent for remembering how to play just about any song. In a lot of ways, playing on a cruise ship is the perfect place for him to be.

51

Kate decides to play along and see where the night takes her. She points to herself and says, "Kate. From New York. My friend is out stargazing but will be along soon."

"Ah! New York!" he says. "Pretty city, but how come your friend just left you here? Male friend, like boyfriend?"

"Female friend. No boyfriend."

"Nice to meet you, Kate, without a boyfriend, from New York. What can I play for you?"

"Oh, anything Barry Manilow!" Kate loves everything from the American songwriter and singer.

Sam bows his head, pretending disappointment.

"The lovely young lady wants to hear Barry Manilow. What a travesty!"

Kate laughs, then squeals in excitement as Sam lays his fingers on the keys.

He starts to play "Mandy" when a voice from the back of the room shouts out, "How about 'Runaway'? She can relate to that one!" That voice! Kate would recognize it anywhere. It sends a shiver throughout her body.

She turns around to see Luca sitting in a swivel chair about twenty feet behind her. Sam is equally surprised. "Luca? Is that you, man? Hey, come on up here. I haven't seen you in forever!" Luca gets up and takes a seat on the other side of the piano, across from Kate.

Something stirs in Kate as she blurts out, "On further reflection, perhaps 'You're So Vain' would be a better choice, Sam."

Sam feels the tension between the two of them.

"I see you two know each other. Sorry to hear about Silvie, Luca. Nikolai told me."

"Yeah, it is what it is, Sam. You know women; they do not know how good they have it, then they leave." Luca looks straight at Kate then down at his drink. Kate notices something sad in his eyes. He gulps down the last sips of alcohol and winces.

"Can I get another?" Luca holds up his glass. The bartender brings him and Sam another round of drinks.

In her seat, Kate turns back to look at Sam, being sure not to look in Luca's direction. In an unfamiliar but exciting way, she's feeling spunky and won't let Luca ruin her night.

"So, Sam, where did you learn to play so well? Or is it a natural-born talent?"

"I picked up a lot of tricks on my travels...studied under street performers as well as maestros. I remember my father played tunes on the old piano when I was younger."

"Ah, I see. I hope you can teach me some tricks too." *Did I just say that?* she muses.

"Sure. I would love to. Do you play?"

"Oh, no. I just like to listen."

Luca is uncharacteristically silent as the conversation continues. He rolls his eyes at Kate's attempt at flirtation while also being annoyed when Sam responds in equal parts admiration and charm. Thinking enough is enough, Luca finally comes over and sits behind Kate. She doesn't acknowledge his presence. He taps her on the shoulder—a grave mistake. Kate spins around and charges like a bull at a toreador's cape.

"What?" she spits out, fire in her eyes and voice.

"Whoa! What's with the attitude?"

"Seriously?"

"Oh, I know; you want a second chance."

Kate cuts him off before he can say another word. "You're disgusting!" She spins back around to face Sam again. She can feel her blood boiling and knows her face is probably bright red.

"I can be as disgusting as I want. I am single."

Kate huffs at the comment. She would rather be anywhere on the ship but here. She picks up her purse, drops a twenty-dollar bill in Sam's tip jar, and, without looking at Luca, says, "As long as you're

53

happy." She spins away from the piano and leaves the lounge to go look for Claudia.

Luca watches her walk away and, in a mocking tone, says to Sam, "As long as you're happy, as long as you're happy. Ah, women! *Perché devono essere così difficili?*" He punctuates the question by slamming his drink.

Sam laughs at the apparent frustration and answers. "Women aren't difficult, my friend. You just need to handle them with care... and leave them be when they've clearly had enough of you!"

"Not helping right now."

Luca rises from his stool to run after Kate but sits back down when Sam's advice finally registers in his mind. "Okay, I will give her time to cool off."

Sam smiles. "See, you're already learning. Another drink?"

⌒

Kate finds herself on the top deck. Not brave enough to walk over to the railing, she sees a lounge chair close to the wall and sits down. The deck is dark and the sky lit up with stars. Kate lies down and soaks in the immenseness of the night sky.

So many thoughts are going through her head. Why did she walk away? She was there first, enjoying the piano music. She should have just ignored him. For the rest of the cruise, she will just ignore him; that's it.

Normally she would text G, and they would chat back and forth over nothing in particular. He always knows when she needs a distraction. He sends her funny pictures or picks on the Yankees to get her to argue with him. And before she knows it, whatever is bothering her is a distant memory. But out at sea, she does not have that option.

Feeling determined to keep moving forward, she looks up at the sky and takes a deep breath.

"I can do this. Can't I?" she asks herself. "I guess I don't really have a choice, do I?"

She takes another deep breath as memories begin to resurface again. A tear rolls down her cheek when she remembers the time when she and Peter were dating. They used to go to a park near campus, and at night they would lie next to each other, staring up at the sky and talking about their future. He proposed to her in that same park.

Talking to the sky, thinking of Peter, she says out loud, "We were supposed to grow old together. I don't think I will ever fully understand why you did what you did. I wish I could talk to you and let you know I am sorry that I failed you."

The tears are flowing now, but she continues, directing her voice upward. "Chelsea is doing well, but I guess you see her, and you know. She misses you." She mourns the loss of her husband quietly in those moments, gazing up at the sky. She mourns for all the moments they won't share together and the life that was only half-built—with Kate left to wonder and wander alone forevermore.

Suddenly, Kate hears someone coming. She sits up, wipes her tears, and puts on a smile. A small group of passengers walks by. Kate recognizes a woman from the morning class. She walks past Kate and smiles.

"Hello, dear," she says. Stopping briefly, she tells her group she will meet up with them in a bit. "Mind if I join you for a minute?"

"Oh, of course. I was just getting some fresh air and enjoying the sky. I don't see stars like this often."

"I know it is beautiful. I wanted to tell you I was so impressed at how you and Luca danced. I would have thought you were a couple."

"Oh, thank you. It was all him. He is an amazing dancer."

A comfortable silence falls between them as the woman sits on a lounge chair next to Kate's.

"I'm Victoria, by the way."

"Nice to meet you, Victoria. I'm Kate."

"Yes, I remember. You are a widow, yes?"

"Yes, I am. How did you know?"

"The look on your face reminds me of the look I wore for many years after my husband died."

"I'm sorry for your loss. Do we know each other from somewhere? Something about you seems so familiar."

"Thank you. No, I don't think so. This is my first voyage on this line. Perhaps it is the sisterhood of widows you're feeling. No one really understands like someone who has been through it."

"That's for sure. How long has it been for you? If you don't mind me asking."

"Oh, it's completely alright. It has been almost fifteen years now since my Peter died."

"Peter?" Kate asks, thinking she must have heard wrong.

"Yes, my husband. I still think about him. The pain eases, but it never goes away."

"I understand that. My husband's name was Peter too."

"Ah, that must be the connection. I'm sure he would want you to know he's sorry about the accident. There was nothing you could have done to stop it."

Kate feels as if she is talking to Peter. She has never mentioned to anyone how Peter died. Claudia, Chelsea, and a few family members are the only ones who know.

There's silence again, then Victoria speaks up, her voice heavy with emotion but still firm. "You know, sometimes I feel my Peter is looking at me from heaven. Do you feel the same way?"

"Sometimes. I would like to think so."

"Kate, I am sure he is looking down at you, even right now as we speak. He wouldn't want you to be unhappy. He would want you to move on. There's nothing you could have done to help him or prevent what happened. Some things are just not in our hands. But some things are."

"I know, but it's so difficult. Every morning, I wake up...I feel sad...I force myself to look for the good, and then I feel I'm cheating on his memory."

"Oh, honey, there's a wonderful feeling in letting go. He would want that. Give him the peace he wants. He couldn't have done anything to stop what happened."

Kate sniffles. Her eyes are full of tears, but she refuses to let them stream down her face.

"Let go, dearie," Victoria whispers comfortingly.

Kate looks at her, smiles and nods, unable to find her voice.

FIVE

The next morning, while Claudia is still asleep, Kate decides to find a nice spot on the middle deck to tackle her rewrite. She left her friend a note the night before, explaining that she went to bed early and hoped Claudia had a nice time stargazing. She would catch up with her the following day. She really doesn't want to have to explain what had happened.

She finds a table off to the side, fairly secluded, but where she can enjoy the sun and the view. She pulls out her *Sleep Naked* notebook and puts in her ear pods for some mood music. She writes something, scribbles it out, writes something else, and scribbles that out, too.

She does this for close to five minutes, not feeling the writing. In frustration, she rips the page out, crumples it up, and starts over. This goes on until Kate realizes she has amassed a nice little pile of failed writing attempts.

Disheartened, she puts down her pen and paper and, remembering that the universe likes specifics, says in a hushed tone, "Okay, Universe, let's try this again. Thank you for sending me the inspiration to steam up my soon-to-be-published book, *Sleep Naked*."

She opens her eyes, cranks up the music, and starts to write again, not noticing that Luca is walking toward her. Once he gets close, he casts a shadow over her form. She looks up. Taking out her ear pods, she looks him in the eyes, saying nothing.

After a surprisingly *not* awkward silence, he finally speaks. "What if I am not?"

"Not what?"

"Happy. You said twice to me yesterday, 'As long as you are happy.' And I do not think I am. *Sono spiacente*. I am sorry I was not nice to you."

Suddenly every angry feeling she has toward Luca is gone.

"How come you're not happy?" she asks.

Luca sits down. He looks out over the water then up to the sky and says, "I am, how you say, a shithead."

Kate laughs but soon realizes he is serious.

"The night I met you, I had just found out that a former lover—the woman I had been in a relationship with for two years—had become engaged to marry another man. I do not know what...I had all kinds of emotions running through me. My first thought was to not go to work, but then the thought of being alone was worse. So, I went in and met you."

"Me, uh, leaving the way I did, didn't come at a good time then?"

"It was not just Silvie. I am thirty-five years old, and I have ruined every relationship I have ever had. I am sorry I was such an ass to you yesterday."

She looks at him for a few seconds before deciding that the man is being earnest.

"Apology accepted."

They both sit there for a minute. Kate doesn't know what to say. She had met Peter in college; they got engaged right before graduation and married the next year. She has no experience being in other relationships, no advice to give to him. Luca has a very pained look on his face, and now Kate realizes what caused the sadness she saw in his eyes the night before.

Luca turns to Kate and, with a most sincere expression, asks her, "Are you happy?"

Kate takes a minute before she answers. She has always considered herself a happy person—and that happiness comes from within. Even despite losing Peter, she remains happy in most areas of her life.

"Yes, I am," she says.

"Are you married?"

"No, but I was. He passed away three years ago."

"I am sorry. You were in love, yes?"

"Absolutely."

Luca again stares out to the water as if searching for what to say.

"I thought I loved each one of them. I would say 'I love you'; she would, too. But after a certain amount of time, I would become an asshole and ruin it, and she would leave."

Again, Kate has no experience with failed relationships. The love she felt for Peter was consuming. They rarely fought, and when they did, they worked it out and their love seemed all the stronger for it. They always talked about what their golden years would be like, so the last year of his life, and his death, had shaken Kate to her core.

"Do you love yourself?"

"You mean, like, take care of Mr. Happy?"

Kate chuckles, then quickly realizes she needs to explain. "No, I mean, do you love yourself, all of you?" She makes a broad gesture with her hands.

"Hell, no. I am an ass."

Kate starts to glimpse what is troubling Luca. "Maybe that is where you need to start. In my opinion, you need to love yourself before you can give your love to another."

61

Kate notices that Luca is growing uncomfortable. Something she said has hit a nerve, so much so that he wants to change the conversation.

"What is all this?" he asks, gesturing at the pile of crumpled-up paper.

Kate sighs, "This...this is my mess. I wrote a book about steamy sex that got rejected because it wasn't steamy enough. That's why I am here, to have sex." Kate is amazed that less than twelve hours ago she was calling this man, with whom she'd almost had sex, disgusting; now she is opening up and telling him her sad story.

"Seriously?" Intrigued, he picked up her notebook.

Kate may have felt comfortable telling Luca her plan, but she is not at all comfortable having him read her writing. She raises her voice in protest. "Hey, give that back!"

Luca ignores her, gets up, and starts to walk a few feet away. "This is good." His approval quiets Kate for a minute. Then he reads some more. "Oh, I see why they tell you that."

The rejection letter fills her thoughts again, and she doesn't want to hear it from yet another person, who certainly is a good judge of steamy sex. She rises to retrieve her notebook.

"Okay, smart guy, I know it needs work. That's why—"

He cuts her off. "You come looking for me." He holds the notebook just out of her reach.

"Ugh, I admit I may have followed you, but I wasn't planning on what happened there to happen. That is what the cruise is for." She's not making any sense, and he looks at her in a questioning way.

"The cruise was so I could have some fun and experiment and not have to worry about running into that person again." She now realizes the ridiculousness of what she is saying.

"That fired back, no?"

"Backfired, *si*." She gets a kick out of his English.

"*Si*...if my charms do not work, I do not know what will." There's that confidence that Kate now calls out as being arrogant.

"*Okay!*" she shouts. Kate is tired of this conversation, and Luca quickly realizes he has overstepped the line.

"Sorry. I tell you I am an ass." As if somehow, that is a good enough reason.

Kate has a change of heart and isn't buying it. "Then who showed up at the group class and was nice to me and the others?"

That comment catches Luca off guard. No one has ever said he was nice. Mostly they say he's arrogant, cocky, and condescending. And a talented dancer. And an egomaniac. He doesn't disagree. With all these thoughts running through his head, he starts to say something, then stops, then starts again, and stops. Finally, "I do not know who that was? That was new for me. I hate teaching, especially group classes, for beginners. But I saw you in the crowd and wanted to have some fun, so I asked Nikolai to let me teach, knowing I would get back at you for leaving me the other night. Then something...something felt different when you walked over, and I heard your name. I just wanted to dance and enjoy myself, with no plan."

Kate wants to speak, but Luca is not finished, so she lets him keep talking. "And I had fun. I relaxed. I was just me. I cannot explain it. That was all new for me."

They sit in silence for a minute, Kate wanting to make sure Luca has a chance to explore his feelings and talk about them if he wants. She knows letting unexpressed feelings ramble around inside of you is not healthy.

When she is sure he's done, she draws on her own struggles and offers him some advice. "Maybe you should explore that further and see why you let that hold you back. Or, if it's not working, maybe it's some thinking that needs to change. Life is an ever-evolving process, and what once worked for you may not any longer." She feels a pang as she says those words, knowing she should follow her own advice.

Luca absorbs her words as if something she said spoke to his soul. "You are very wise, dear Kate."

"I read a lot, and I've been through a lot." That's an understatement. "But just not enough steamy sex, they say. And I guess the more I think about it, I'm not ready yet either."

Luca smiles. There's a glint in his eye that suggests he has a fantastic plan, something Kate is going to either love or be wary of. "I have an idea. Sex is my forte; love seems to be yours. For the next four days, you help me figure out my love problem, and I will help you steam up your book."

Kate is not sure what to say, but Luca puts her mind at ease. "I will be a perfect gentleman. Hands to myself. I promise to be a Boy Scout. What do you say?"

He asks the question as if she has a choice, but Luca assumes she will agree. He picks up her stuff and adds, "I even throw in some dance lessons. Fix a few things."

Kate stands up as she realizes he is going to walk away with her stuff. What's worse, she takes issue with his crack about dance lessons.

"Fix a few things?" she roars. "I thought you said I was a good dancer."

They continue their conversation as they walk along the deck.

"You are good, but why settle for good when you could be great?"

———

Kate has run back to her cabin to grab her shoes. She changes into them while Luca sifts through the music on her phone. The last of the group class is now leaving the ballroom. He always finds that his students—and Kate is now his, as he is hers—dance better to music they love. As he searches her song list, he notices that he and Kate have similar taste in music, everything from big band classics to Motown, dance, and pop. He also notices she has several playlists and finds the titles interesting: Running Tunes, Keep Moving, Show-Dance Songs, Stop Crying, Writing Music, and Find Your Purpose.

Luca realizes he is looking at a snapshot of Kate's life. He smiles at the thought, yet he is curious to know more about the woman who has agreed to dance with him again, albeit grudgingly.

"Okay, let us get steamy!" Luca claps his hands, rubs them together, and walks over to Kate. He bows slightly and asks, "May I have this dance?"

Kate can't imagine anyone turning him down. For some reason, she pictures him in a tuxedo and decides he must look devilishly handsome. He has picked a rumba, one of her favorite dances. Rumba gives the dancers a chance to be flirty and stylish, and there are so many great songs that fit a rumba. In her head, Kate quickly tries to remember everything Max, her dance instructor in New York, has ever told her about rumba. Slow, quick, quick, slow was the timing. Stand tall, chin up, knees bent, toes turned in slightly. Don't pick your feet up. Relax. Relax? That's a good one.

Luca walks over to her, and the first thing he does is lift her chin and pull her shoulders back. "Posture is everything. Present yourself. Chin up, shoulders back, tits out. You have got them; flaunt them." How does this man make her blush so much?

They begin dancing, but Kate is thinking about the dance's technicalities and rules, anything except being in the moment and having fun. Luca notices this and stops the dance midway.

"Okay, what is happening with you?"

"What?" she responds, thinking she is doing everything right.

"Where is the girl from the club? Or yesterday?"

"Again, what?"

"You feel different, stiff."

Oh, here we go again, she thinks before attempting to explain. "I'm a little nervous."

"Nervous? It is just..."

"Oh, I hate that word!" she explodes.

"What word?"

"*Just.* Just blah blah blah. Why can't you just blah blah blah? Never knew how for forty-seven years, so I'll just start right now. *Ugh!*"

"You are forty-seven?"

Kate exhales in frustration. *Is that all he got from the tirade?* she wonders. She is tempted to say, "Forget it. Have a nice life," but she doesn't. She can't even move, since Luca is holding her.

He feels her frustration. He's seen it a thousand times in the span of only a few meetings. "*Scusi,* I mean you do not look like you are forty-seven. Why are you nervous? You had my tongue in your mouth a few nights ago."

Somehow the ridiculousness of that statement makes Kate laugh and relax a bit. "Because I know you are a freakin' professional ballroom dancer, and an arrogant one too. And you're going to start picking apart every little thing I should do but don't. I cannot relax because I have a gazillion things to remember, and I don't know how to be that girl from the club again. I think that was that one night. That isn't me, and—" she stops in midsentence. "Why are you smiling?!"

How dare he smile at her when she is having a meltdown!

"You know you are adorable when you are doing the freaking out," Luca chuckles. "Okay, I have an idea. Come with me."

He picks up her things again and starts walking toward the door, expecting her to follow him. She does, not 100 percent sure why, but she does. A short distance away is the lounge where they argued last night. The piano is silent, and there is no one in here except one lonely bartender.

Luca puts Kate's things down on a chair off to the side of the little dance floor. He walks over to the bar and returns with four shots. "Salute!" He hands Kate one glass before holding his own to the air.

"Salute!" Kate says, and she slams her shot. She promptly coughs and declares, "I'm not much of a shots person, but wow! I feel all warm and tingly."

Watching her makes Luca smile.

"Do you know what makes a dancer great?" he inquires of her.

"Skills," she instantly replies, to which he shakes his head no.

"Skills are important, *si*, and make a dancer good, but passion is what makes a dancer great. When you have passion for something, you give it all you have, leave yourself out there, and not care what anyone thinks. You need to *feel* the music, not just listen to it. Respond to it and create a perfect blend of skills and passion."

"Oh, boy, that's not going to be easy for me." She reaches for another shot and downs it, then coughs again.

Luca gives her a sly smile. "And you do not find your passion at the bottom of a shot glass."

"You don't?" Kate asks, remembering that most of her courage comes in liquid form.

"No, you find it here." He puts his finger on her heart. The fact that he brushes her chest ever so slightly sends a quiver through Kate's body.

"But what about the voices up here?" she says as she points to her head. "The ones that tell you to ignore your passion and do what's safe or do what others want you to do." Kate can't fathom following her passion. She is sensible, reliable, safe.

Luca has an easy answer for her. "You tell them to fuck off!" Kate wasn't expecting that and almost snorts a laugh. He continues expounding his theory: "When you dance, your purpose is not to get to a certain spot on the floor but to enjoy it every step of the way."

"It's not that easy," replies Kate, thinking back to all the times she has played it safe. The night in London was probably the only time she ever let go and gave in to her desires. But a lifetime of living safely doesn't erase itself that easily.

Luca reminds her again, "Stop thinking so much." At this point, he pulls her up and holds her in an almost embrace, then starts to sway to the music. "Close your eyes."

"Excuse me?"

"Close your eyes."

67

"How will I know where I'm going?"

"You do not need to know. You are the follower, so your job is to respond to where I direct you to go. Not to anticipate, not to question, just, um, only go. You have to let everything else go." The song "Breathe" by Faith Hill is playing. Kate closes her eyes.

I can feel the magic floating in the air
Being with you gets me that way
I watch the sunlight dance across your face
And I've never been this swept away.

The dreaminess of the song combines with the proximity to Luca and the two shots to relax Kate. Luca's voice echoes in her head: "I think now you do not care who I am, or what I know, or what anyone thinks. So go with that." He's right for the most part, but she definitely cares about him. A lot.

Luca dances slowly with Kate as she loses herself in the lyrics.

Cause I can feel you breathe
It's washing over me
And suddenly I'm melting into you
There's nothing left to prove
Baby, all we need is just to be
Caught up in the touch
Slow and steady rush
Baby, isn't that the way love's supposed to be
I can feel you breathe, just breathe.

Luca is in total control. Kate, for once, is going with the flow, enjoying the dance, the closeness, the warmth. As the song ends, Luca sends her back into a long dip. She comes back up, opens her eyes. They are face-to-face. Luca opens his mouth. He is so close. Kate's head is spinning. He whispers, "Now that is more like it." His smile radiates through her body, and she exhales about ten years' worth of things she was holding on to.

"That is more fun. I don't think I can put into words how amazing that felt to just be moving; not looking, thinking, just moving." She feels like she is in a dream. It is not until a group of noisy passengers bursts into the room that they let go of each other, long after the music has ended.

SIX

After the dance lesson, Kate and Luca step out onto the deck to enjoy the weather. They talk and walk, savoring each other's company and not really wanting to end their time together. Strolling along the deck, admiring the beautiful scenery, Luca finally broaches the subject of love. Although he is a bit hesitant at first, slowly he decides to be vulnerable with Kate, to talk about the subject many think about but don't say out loud: love, the elusive puzzle piece of his life.

"How do you know you are in love?" he asks helplessly. "How did *you* know?"

Kate takes a moment before she responds. Despite his tough, womanizing exterior, Luca clearly yearns for love. "I think it's different for everyone. For me, I knew—and I know it sounds odd, but you'll know when you know. You may have thought you felt it a hundred times, but the one time it is meant to be, it feels different than all the rest."

He looks skeptical, but as Kate continues talking, the lines in his forehead disappear.

"When I was pregnant with my daughter," Kate recalls, "a lady in my birthing class asked, 'How do you know when you're in labor?' The nurse in charge of the class said you'll know. We all kinda looked around like, uh, we don't think we will. She explained that there are many false alarms—cramps, kicks, and all other sorts of things that make you think you are in labor—but there is a moment when you realize it's not a false alarm. Hey, this is the real thing. She was just, like, you'll know."

He's still not buying it, she can tell. "Not a good example if you have never given birth. Back to me, I just wanted to be with him all the time, and when I wasn't, I was thinking about him and when I would see him again. I would light up when he came into the room. Everything about him, about being with him, was just...easy."

"Is that not what it is like at the beginning for everyone?"

"Maybe. In my case, though, it never faded. It lasted the whole time. And for people that are together years and years and years, they'll tell you the same. There are times when things get tough, but when that person has your heart, you figure out how to work through the tough times. It was not an option *not* to work it out. You'd do anything for someone you love."

Luca senses there is more to what she's saying than her words suggest. He wants to ask about the times when things didn't work. He wants to know about her and her life until the day they met at the London club. He starts to say something, but he doesn't know how to phrase it. What can he possibly ask? "Tell me about your relationship with your husband who died, who you seem to have loved more than life itself. But now he's not here but you are?" Suddenly his problem doesn't seem so major. In fact, maybe the fear of losing a love that big is the reason he doesn't look for it.

From the expressions on his face, she can tell there must be a thousand thoughts racing through his mind. His eyes give it away every time.

"What is it?" she asks, hoping he'll open up.

He starts to say, "I," but he catches himself and settles for, "That must be a wonderful feeling to have that with someone."

"Yes, it is, but when you lose it...when you lose the love of your life, everything changes. It is the worst feeling in the world." Kate stops for a second then continues, "As hard as it is, though, I would never want to *not* have experienced it." She wants Luca to know that he should not be afraid of experiencing the same. In the end, loving somebody with all your heart and soul is definitely worth the risk of them leaving you one day: "Isn't it better to have loved and lost than not to have loved at all?"

Luca stays silent, lost in his thoughts.

Knowing that sometimes too much information clouds your thoughts and mind, Kate decides to shelve the conversation for the time being. Anyway, such thoughts make her go back to the time when she felt that, somehow, she had failed Peter. And she wants to avoid that feeling.

"Okay, my turn!" she says playfully. "I know sex isn't like they show it in the movies. The angles don't make sense. It just seems so unrealistic."

"I do not know about that. Maybe you just have not been with someone who knows what they are doing." He instantly regrets saying that, not wanting to diminish her husband's ability. However, it doesn't seem to bother her.

"I guess that's possible. About a year after my husband died, I went out on a date with someone I was flirty with and, well, it got to that point, and I didn't, you know, I didn't..."

"Did not what?"

"You know, I didn't have a...you know." The fact that she has a hard time being open about her sexuality should be a clue to someone trying to write a steamy adult fiction story. Kate has all she can do to not crawl into a hole at this very moment.

73

"Kate, you are forty-seven years old, my dear," Luca reasons. "It is okay to say 'orgasm.'"

Now Kate is really embarrassed. Wanting desperately to move on from having to say the word, she defends herself. "Anyway, I used to have them all the time—I mean *all* the time." She wants that known for some reason. "I feel like I lost something." Her tone turns from embarrassed to downtrodden. "I think it meant I wasn't ready, and that I'm not meant to write steamy adult fiction."

Luca is determined to make sure she does not give up on her dream. You regret giving up at some point. He knows. "I am not so sure about that." He reaches for her hands, does a fancy spin move, pulls her in, and rolls her back and around for a slow, sensual dip. Kate forgets all about the discussion.

They find themselves in a quiet, almost deserted part of the ship, moving in sync, so close. Kate is totally comfortable being this close to this very sexy man. The outside world no longer exists. All she wants is to stay like this a little bit longer. And maybe the memories of her past will melt away and not resurface in her mind.

That night at dinner, Kate and Claudia are sitting with Luca and Nikolai. Their table is on the outer edge of the raised middle seating area. They are laughing and enjoying themselves. One older gentleman walks by and asks jokingly, "How do I get a seat at the kiddie table?" To most of the other passengers, the four of them are youngsters.

Claudia looks around. "I guess we are the youngest passengers." She also takes the time to stir up some trouble, as only Claudia can. "So...no word from G here out at sea?"

Kate gives her friend a why-would-you-bring-him-up look and rolls her eyes. Hoping to downplay it, she quickly says, "Uh, no...no signal, I'm sure." She tries to change the topic of conversation, but she's too slow and it's too late. Luca heard it.

"Who is G?" he asks. He is looking at Kate, who looks everywhere but at him before finally landing her eyes on the man.

"Just a friend," she replies.

"Friend, my ass!" Claudia laughs, intent on stirring up something. "Do 'just friends' look at each other like this?" Claudia pulls out her phone and searches for the picture of G and Kate at her birthday party a year ago. She captured them in the middle of a slow dance, looking at each other rather intently. She shows Nikolai and Luca the photo.

Kate eagerly wants to defuse this conversation. Yes, she *had* feelings—past tense—for G; and yes, they stemmed from a long time ago. But *no*...she no longer feels them. At least that's what she has to keep telling herself.

"She always brings this up when she's had too much to drink," Kate stammers. "She doesn't know what she's talking about."

Claudia and Nikolai, thankfully, have moved on to talk about something in London. Kate is happy to have that conversation over.

"I do not know about that," Luca muses. "I think I have to agree with Claudia. Eyes are the mirror to the soul."

Kate agrees with Luca on that, but not her feelings for G. "Well, think what you want, but he's my attorney. He'll help me negotiate my book deal if...I mean when. And we are friends—friends for a *long* time. We grew up across the street from each other, went to school together, but we lost touch after high school. He went his way; I went mine." She hopes this rehearsed speech will be the end of the conversation.

Luca, however, isn't letting it go.

"So, what is the reason nothing happened between you two?"

Hoping to lay it all out there and be done with it, Kate turns to Luca. "Our parents moved to the same neighborhood when we were both babies. We did everything together, but once we got to around third grade, he became the popular one and I was the shy one. We were in different friend groups, and the gap just got wider the older we got. After graduation, we went on to new things. He went to law school after college and became an attorney; I met Peter in college, and we got married soon after graduation. We didn't stay in touch, and I only got updates when I would see his mom. But when Peter died, he was there for me like a good friend would be. In the beginning, I am sure his mom made him, but over time he pushed me to go out; he made me laugh, took care of some business things. He..." Kate searches for the right words to explain what G means to her, but she decides to go in a different direction. "Well, let's just say I'm not his type." She reaches for her wine glass, suddenly in need of a big drink.

"His type is not pretty, fun, smart, sweet, and loving?"

Kate laughs. "Actually, no! His type is super-hot, not so bright. His relationships don't really last very long."

Luca feels that, and now he too wants a change of scenery and conversation. "His loss! Come on, let us go dancing." He stands up and extends a hand to Kate. Luca announces to the rest of the group, "We are going to the ballroom. You guys coming?" He secretly hopes, however, that everyone will decline. He just wants another chance to hold Kate.

Sure enough, nobody seated at the table is interested in going to the ballroom, so Luca and Kate say their goodbyes and leave. There is a brief silence when Nikolai remarks to no one in particular, "Wow!" He is shocked by his friend's behavior.

Curious, Claudia asks, "What?"

"I'm not sure what effect your friend has," Nikolai explains. "I've not seen Luca *want* to dance in a long time."

"She is pretty special. Why would he not want to dance? Isn't he a world champion or something?"

Nikolai hesitates to talk about Luca, but figures maybe it's time for Luca to face his past. And this woman might be the key to unlocking that for him. What better way than to tell Claudia, hoping it gets back to Kate. "He's had a pretty interesting life. His parents taught ballroom dance in Italy. He had a very normal life until around twelve, I think it was, when his little sister died. She was only six."

Knowing the heartbreak of losing a loved one, Claudia feels his pain.

"I don't think he ever got over it," Nikolai continues. "His whole life changed at that moment. He was angry at the world. His parents had such a void. They pushed him and pushed him to be a champion. He never got to have a normal childhood. I don't think dancing was his dream, but he did it for his parents."

"I guess that is reason enough not to enjoy it."

"The hard part was that he was so talented, but he didn't enjoy it. He ended up losing his passion for it. I can only imagine if he had loved it....He and his partner won just about everything, but their relationship imploded, I think partly from the pressure to always be excellent. But also, in part, because his heart wasn't in it."

While Claudia and Nikolai are chatting away in the dining room, Kate and Luca venture to the ballroom. Live music fills the air. Couples are dancing around the floor, men and women dressed elegantly, swaying in time. After Kate finishes putting on her dance shoes, Luca extends a hand and asks, "Ready to show off?"

"Pretty sure that is not how anyone would ever describe me." But she reluctantly takes his hand and rises to her feet. Luca's confidence is contagious.

"Good time to change that. *Andiamo*!"

Luca leads her to the middle of the dance floor. The song "Someone Like You" is being played by the band. Luca holds Kate firmly as if to say everything is all right. They sway back and forth as Luca feels the music. Kate looks down at the floor, showing her nervousness. Luca tugs at the back of her hair, forcing her to look up—right into his eyes. Her nerves steady. He waits for the right moment, and off they go around the dance floor. It's not long before the other couples stop to watch.

The song lyrics fill her head:

I've been searching a long time
Someone exactly like you
I've been traveling all around the world
Waiting for you to come through
Someone like you makes it all worthwhile
Someone like you keeps me satisfied
Someone exactly like you.

In addition to the lyrics and dreamy melody, Kate hears Luca talking to her throughout the dance: "Reach...breathe...become one with the music...get lost in it...have no fear! You know where you are going. *Go!*"

One dance turns into another, and another, and another. Kate is on such an emotional high that her smile lights up the room. She has not felt this way in such a long time. She sits down to have a drink and rest a bit. As much fun as she is having, Luca is pushing her to dance bigger than she ever has, so it's a little tiring. Luca, on the other hand, is reborn. It's as if his "live life" switch has flipped on again.

"What do you say we move this to the lounge?" he asks. "I am in the mood for different music."

Kate, too, is ready to slow things down a bit. They walk down a hallway to make their way to the lounge.

"I don't think I would ever have that much fun dancing again," she says. "*Grazie*, Luca."

"*Prego*! It helps to have the right partner." He winks at her.

"I suppose...for dance, sex, and love." She gives her attempt at a wink, but it looks goofy.

"I will teach you how to wink too." That makes Kate smile.

"What are you thinking about?" He sees the look in her eyes.

"Winking makes me think of one of my favorite books, *When God Winks*."

"Hmm."

"What hmm?"

"I am mad at God for taking my baby sister. She got sick and died at an early age. There was no reason for that."

They walk in silence for a minute. Kate surely knows what it feels like to lose someone and not understand the enormity of it. There really are no words to say, other than "I can understand." And they keep walking until they reach the lounge.

The crowd at the lounge is pretty thin, just a few people milling around the bar. The piano is silent. With a drink and a change of scenery, Luca regains his enthusiasm. "What I was hoping for! We have the dance floor to ourselves!"

He pulls out his phone and heads to the sound system behind the piano. Kate watches him plug in this, unplug that, adjust some dials, and suddenly the room comes alive with music that makes her head spin. If you had told her three years ago that she would be on a cruise in Europe, dancing and flirting to her heart's content with a handsome, sexy, Italian ballroom dancer, she would have thought you were crazy. But here she is—plus she's getting valuable information for her book. It'll be a bestseller for sure. *That is one doozy of a wink, God*, she thinks.

She must be in a trance, because she doesn't see Luca walk back over to her. He extends a hand with the sexiest "My lady" as he spins her out, wraps her back into a tight embrace, then slowly starts to sway back and forth. Every time he smiles at her, she melts. Almost as amazing is how totally relaxed she feels with him. Just earlier, she was nervous and fidgety. Now she feels confident, fearless. She is living in the moment.

They dance non-stop for another two hours, stopping only to drink and chat. He even stops and corrects something in her dancing, and she welcomes the advice with the words "Why be good when you can be great?" echoing in her head.

Finally, the bartender gets their attention by loudly clearing his throat. "Sorry, folks, we're closing for the evening. Hope to see you back tomorrow."

"But we just started!" Kate whines like a ten-year-old leaving Disney World.

"No problem," Luca comforts. "We can dance tomorrow. Let us go get some air. *Andiamo.*"

At midnight, the ship's deck is pretty much deserted. Luca takes Kate's hand, spins her around, and brings her in for a long, slow dip. It's obvious that both of them are turned on at this moment. How can she not be, dancing with a handsome man, his eyes fixed on her? And for Luca, being with Kate is like watching a flower bloom, and he knows he is partly responsible for that.

When he holds her tight, she fits right in next to him. Her warmth radiates to him. And he cannot overlook her yoga-sculpted body with its exquisite breasts. How is he going to control himself? *Damn that Boy Scout promise!* he tells himself.

As Kate arches back away from him, he hears her say, "I love dips."

"Now, push your hips up toward me," he replies, wanting to fulfill her wish.

Kate giggles.

"Someone has a dirty mind," he says.

"Yes, I do," she purrs, "and I'm not afraid to use it." Luca pulls her back up until they are so very close. Kate tenses up a bit and backs away, collecting herself. "Unfortunately, I am also an ATNA, so I don't usually get too far."

"ATNA?" He scrunches his eyebrows in confusion.

"ATNA: All Talk, No Action."

Luca ponders the phrase for a moment. "I have not heard of that before, but now that I think about it, I know a few ATNAs."

"G is the one who introduced me to the term. He says I am the queen of ATNA."

"Ah, the mysterious G! What does he say you are ATNA about?"

"Pretty much everything. He says I always run my mouth about wanting to do things but never do, hence the term."

"Why do you not take action on something and send him a photograph to prove it."

Kate contemplates what Luca has said. G is always picking on her for saying all the things she wants to do but never following through. What's one thing that would make his head spin? As if a lightbulb went off over her head, she pulls out her phone, opens the camera, turns it around, and points it at the two of them like she is going to take a picture. Luca doesn't understand what is so daring about taking a picture, but he smiles. Kate holds up the camera with one hand and with the other touches Luca's chin ever so slightly to turn his face toward her. Then she kisses him, snaps a picture, and steps back proudly.

"ATNA no more!" she says defiantly. "I'll send it to him tomorrow when we get to port. *Ha!*" She is proud of herself—and the kiss felt nice too. She felt him kiss her back. It was an equally amazing feeling. His lips were so soft. And he smelled so good.

Luca does his best to feign outrage. "I am not sure how I like being used like that. I am not a piece of steak." Kate looks at him, knowing he's not serious. He changes his tune quickly. "On second thought, I'm okay with it." Oh, and he can make her laugh.

Feeling energized, Kate starts contemplating all the other ATNA things on her list. "You know, now that I am knocking ATNAs off, there is one thing I've always been afraid to do, and tomorrow would be perfect, since we will be docking."

"What? Parasailing? Skydiving?"

Kate laughs. "Gosh, no! Baby steps. It may not seem like a big deal, but I want to go swimming in the ocean."

Luca isn't sure he has heard her right. "Um, what?"

"I am super afraid of water: pools, oceans, bridges, boats; I don't even like taking baths. So jumping into the ocean would be huge for me."

"You know, there is a beautiful beach the locals keep hidden from tourists. Water is calm. That would be a good place for you to—how you say?—take the plunger."

Kate loves how he mixes up words. "Perfect! Is it hard to find? My Spanish is a little rusty."

"Not when you have the best tour guide," he says, pointing to himself. "And I know a great spot to have a drink and look at some of the pretty views. We can make a day of it and have lunch."

"That sounds great."

Did she just say yes to a date? On cue, she starts overthinking. And the thinking is followed by a retreat. "Well, I better get some sleep then for my big adventure. Goodnight! Thanks for everything!" She gives Luca a quick kiss on the cheek then scurries off. He watches her disappear around the corner, realizing he has a huge smile on his face and cannot wait to see her tomorrow.

Nikolai is still up when Luca returns to their cabin. Sounding like his father, he says to Luca, "Well, look who finally decided to call it a night. Were you out dancing this whole time, or did you move on to something a little more exciting?"

"Well, if you must know, we danced a lot, and I had a really nice time. And I also do not kiss and tell."

"Yes, you do. Now spill it. What happened?" Nikolai turns into a teenage girl wanting to know all about her best friend's first date.

"Nothing really. Just a kiss. That was it."

"Just a kiss? Is famed ladies' man Luca Bell'Angelo losing his touch?"

"*No!* Not at all; we are just friends. She wanted to make someone be jealous, so she took a picture of us kissing. That is all. If the inquisition is over, I am going to bed. We are going to Biscay tomorrow, so I will be up early."

He climbs into bed.

Nikolai isn't letting it go so easily, though. "Ah, a date, eh? Well, well, well."

"It is not a date. We are going to the beach and maybe get some lunch."

"Ah, beach and lunch..."

Luca throws a pillow at his friend before Nikolai can finish the sentence. Satisfied that Nikolai is quiet, Luca turns over and goes to sleep, thinking of Kate.

SEVEN

The next morning, Kate is waiting in the lounge area with the other early risers, ready to disembark for a day at the beach. She woke up full of spirit and courage, eager to tackle her quest to jump into the ocean. She even arrived a few minutes early to wait for Luca.

In those few minutes, doubt starts to creep into her head.

"G is right," she scolds herself. "You're an ATNA and always will be. What was I thinking? Damn wine and dips." Her instinct to flee kicks in, and she decides to leave before Luca arrives.

"I'll tell him something. He won't care. I'm sure he has better things to do with his time."

The excuses are flowing now. As she turns to head to the exit, she runs right into Luca. Oh, he smells so good!

"You are not being a chicken, are you?" he asks. He knows from the look on her face.

Her awkward denial—"*Me?* No! Let's go!"—doesn't fool anyone. However, Luca isn't about to let her backtrack. As they head off the ship, he holds her hand tightly to make sure she doesn't attempt to flee. And because he likes holding her hand.

He flags a taxi and instructs the driver to take them to Playa de Sopelana. He then turns to Kate to explain the day's events. "I think we should start at the beach while you still have your courage." Kate wonders if she ever really had it, but who could say no to Luca? "Then a quick walk to the cafe. You will love it. Okay?" She can object, but there's no point. It seems as if everything is happening so fast.

"Great," she mutters weakly before rubbing her wishbone necklace. Luca notices the unconscious motion and raises his eyes in curiosity.

"What is that you do with your necklace? I see you do it often."

"Oh, sometimes I don't realize that I do it. My daughter gave me this necklace a few months after my husband died. The story is, you make a wish on it; then one day the string will break, and that means your wish will have been fulfilled."

She pauses for a moment, the memory of that day still fresh. Chelsea understood that her mom was hurting and needed something to hope for, to look forward to. She reminded Kate about her dream to be an author and suggested that she take the opportunity to write, to throw herself into something.

"At the time, I just wanted the pain to go away. I wanted to be happy again. Over the last few years, I've been happy. I mean, I think I am a happy person dealing with life, so I'm not sure why I'm still hanging on to this. I think now I use it when I want to summon up some courage. Then again, I've made so many wishes, I think I've confused it."

"Well, what is one wish?"

She thinks before answering the question. If there is one wish she wanted to come true, it definitely would be to transport herself back to that night in London and not be afraid to have a night of passion that would turn her world upside down and inside out. But she doesn't want to say that out loud, since their arrangement is hands-to-yourself.

Instead, she reveals her other wish: "To be a published author and say what I want, when I want. To be my authentic self. I guess that's a couple of wishes combined."

Luca simply comments, "I understand that more than you know," and they ride the last few minutes in silence.

The taxi drops them off at the beach. Luca, ever the gentleman, carries everything and looks for a quiet place to set up. As they walk along, Kate notices that most of the women are tanned and toned—and topless. She knows she could stand to lose about ten pounds, so being in the vicinity of all these beautiful young women makes her self-conscious. Luca finds a spot, puts down the two towels, then proceeds to take off his shirt. Kate can't help but look.

She remembers running her hands over his chest that night at the club. When he held her tight, she could feel how strong he is. She catches herself staring and quickly turns away to fidget with her things. Luca smiles. He knows she was looking, then pretending not to. He loves that about her. He also knows what she is doing.

"Stop stalling," he playfully chides her.

He takes her things, puts them down. Kate takes a deep breath. Her nerves are in overdrive. She finally agrees, "Okay, let's go." Slowly she starts to walk toward the water, but Luca stops her.

"Not so fast." He tugs at her cover-up. "You do not want to get this wet, do you?"

Kate laughs nervously. "Oh, ha, yeah, silly me. Cause I'll be going *in* the water, right!"

Luca tries to calm her fears. "There is nothing to be afraid of. The water is calm, clear, and I will not let you drown. *Prometto.* I promise."

Kate slowly takes off her cover-up. She has a curvy figure, nothing like the super thin twenty-somethings on the beach.

Luca's eyes go wide as he exclaims in amazement, "*Whoa!* Why would you cover that? Let me see! Turn around!"

Kate is not sure whether to be flattered or embarrassed. She has never been good at accepting compliments. "Oh, stop!" she says playfully.

"At least I do not pretend not to look." He caught her. She waits for that familiar burning feeling of embarrassment to rush to her cheeks, but it never comes. "Sexy does not come from the shape of the body, but the fire in the soul."

"Okay, Socrates, let's go." She tries to laugh it off, but his words have made an impression on her.

Kate begins walking very gingerly toward the water. Luca is puzzled. It's not rocky. Why is she walking so slowly? She is clearly stalling again.

"*Per l'amor del cielo*! For heaven's sake!" Luca scoops her up and makes his way to the water's edge.

Kate is terrified. Her body tenses. She clings to his neck. "Luca, please do not drop me in the water!" Luca is pretty sure that if he lets her go, she will still be wrapped around his neck. That's how tight she is holding on.

"You really are scared. You do not have to be. I will not let you fall."

She relaxes a bit after hearing Luca say those kind words in her ear.

"When I was little, I got knocked over by a wave at the beach. I'm pretty sure I almost drowned. I can still hear in my head how everything was muffled when I was underwater. Since that day, I can't stand the sound of water rushing over my head." She squirms a little, then clings even tighter.

Luca backs out of the water and puts Kate down carefully, still holding on to her to make sure she doesn't make a break for it. She's come so far now. "Okay," he says. "We take it easy, si?" He holds her hand as they slowly, very slowly, wade knee-deep into the water. Kate braces as a tiny wave rolls in. Luca turns his head to hide his smile.

"I can tell you're laughing," she huffs. "I'm trying!"

"Let us promenade out a bit farther." Luca tries relating their current activity to dancing, so he holds her in a promenade position. Their bodies are touching, his right thigh to her left. Their heads are turned to look straight over the water. "And I am only doing this to help. The fact that your leg is touching mine means nothing." She knows it's not true. He is getting turned on holding her like this.

They both smile and laugh, relaxing Kate. They venture out a bit farther.

Kate has relaxed quite a bit by now and is even beginning to enjoy being in the water. "You know, it's not bad after all!" She starts splashing around, focusing on Luca before turning to face the beach. Luca sees a wave runner coming across and realizes its wake is now heading right toward them.

"Uh, Kate, come here for a second."

She is starting to have fun, but the look on his face makes her feel something is wrong.

"Hold on to me," he instructs her.

Kate has no time to react before she feels the wave hit her back. Just like that, the water is over her head. When they come up, Luca quickly checks to make sure that Kate is all right. He pulls her toward him, and they are now face-to-face. He wants to kiss her, but he remembers his promise to be a gentleman and holds himself in check.

Kate realizes what has just happened. She was underwater, and she came back up. It wasn't as scary as she remembered. Being in his arms gave her the courage to want to do more.

"Watch this!" she says as she holds her nose, drops under the water, and springs back up, totally delighted with herself. "I did it! I got wet, all the way wet! I need pictures!"

Kate heads back to the shore to retrieve her phone, with Luca watching her the whole way. He was so close. He wanted to kiss her. He didn't expect to feel like this when he made that promise.

He starts to wade out of the water as she hits the shoreline. Kate hands him her phone with the camera open, almost impatiently. "I need proof! I got wet!" Her face is animated, her wide eyes filled with excitement.

"Okay," he says as he holds up the camera. "But I want it known I am responsible for getting you wet." That remark catches her off guard. She knows what he means has nothing to do with the ocean, and she smiles the most genuinely happy smile just as he takes the picture. She walks toward him, brushes up against him, takes her phone, and lingers for a second.

She whispers in his ear, "The credit is all yours."

Then she walks back to the towels and sits down. Luca joins her, propping himself up on one elbow. She is on her phone, sending G the picture of herself in the water. She notices that he didn't respond to the picture of her kissing Luca the night before.

In this latest photo, Kate is dripping wet and smiling quite seductively, thanks to Luca's comment. The caption reads, "Scaredy cat no more! Look who's all wet." She giggles to herself.

G is quick to respond, "I don't think that proves anything. How do I know it didn't just rain? Maybe an action shot?"

"I'd like to give him a shot, alright." Kate looks at Luca. "He doesn't believe me!"

"There is only one thing to do then." He pulls out his phone, searches his playlist for the song "Geronimo," and leaves his phone playing that song for Kate. "I will to be right back. Listen to this for inspiration." He takes her phone and walks over to a man standing not far from them. He is talking and pointing to Kate. She hears the words to the song:

Well we rushed it
Moving away too fast that we crushed it
But it's in the past
We can make this leap
Through the curtains of the waterfall
So say "Geronimo!"

90

Kate gets an idea of what he has in mind. She stands up as he runs back to her. He grabs her hand, and they both take off for the water. They splash in a few feet, then jump!

When they come up, Kate is beside herself. "*That was amazing!* I've never, *ever* jumped in!" He moves toward her. She throws her arms up in celebration.

"*Grazie*, Luca!"

"*Prego*! You are most welcome."

He cannot wait another moment. He takes her by the hands and pulls her toward him. He kisses her—a long, soft kiss. Kate melts into his arms, turning the soft kiss into a passionate one. The man Luca asked to take the video is keeping the camera on them still.

They back away from each other slowly. Kate licks her lips to taste Luca. They walk back to the towels, not saying a word, both of them silently contemplating what had just happened.

Luca retrieves her phone and hands it to her. He sits down, watching her texting away, sending the video to G. She has a mischievous look on her face.

"What are you thinking?" he inquires of her.

She pauses for a moment. She wants to tell him to kiss her again. But she decides against that. "I always envied the ladies who were comfortable enough to go topless on the beach."

Kate rises to her knees, undoes her bikini top, flings it to the side, and takes a picture of it lying in the sand. She has her back to Luca, but she certainly has his attention. She lies down on her stomach, displaying a proud smile. Luca is mesmerized.

In New York, G walks over to his phone and opens it to see the latest text from Kate. He's ready for another witty exchange. They love to tease each other, and he knows just how far to push it before she gets really mad. It's like when they were little and he teased her, mostly to get her attention. Then they go back and forth until they both laugh and return to whatever they were doing. Only that one time did he go too far.

There was no witty comeback this time, only a video of Kate running toward the water next to a man. "What on earth?" He watches Kate and this man splash into the water, the man diving in, Kate holding her nose and falling backward into the water.

"Wow, she finally did it!" When they come up, G also notices they are very close to each other. He sees the man move forward to kiss Kate. G definitely does not like what he is feeling now. His phone dings again, and this time he sees a black bikini top lying in the sand, along with the caption: "KATE 3, ATNA 0."

The cafe Luca took Kate to is right out of a scene in a movie: high on top of a hill, situated off a square in the middle of a tiny village, surrounded by cobblestone streets lined with shops and restaurants, people and families milling around. From their table outside, they view the fountain in the middle of the square, with the ocean providing a backdrop. Enchanting, to say the least.

"Hey, Luca," Kate asks as she sips a glass of sangria. "I have a question."

"Fire away at me!" Luca replies, proud of his use of an English idiom.

"So...say you're with a woman, and you end up having sex..."

"Ah, one of *those* questions." Luca stiffens in his seat, assuming the proper role of sex professor. He loves these questions. He loves her naivete, her lack of experience. He wants to *show* her the things he tells her about. "Continue."

"You're both done, you both *or-gasmed*," Kate continues, careful to enunciate the last word to show off how she can say it without turning five shades of red.

"Ah, look at you!" Luca was proud of his student. "Next thing you know, you'll be saying 'fuck.'"

Letting that one pass, Kate returns to the topic at hand. "Anyway, as I was saying, now that you're done, how do you decide if you leave or stay? And what if you want to leave and she doesn't?"

Luca studies her for a moment, noticing that his silence is starting to make her squirm. "Are you asking for your book or for yourself?"

"Research for my book, of course."

"Of course." His sexy grin signals he's not buying it. "Well, it depends. I usually leave it to her. If I do not want to deal with it, then I do not bring her back to my place. If I go to her place, then I can decide."

"Good to know—for the book, of course." Kate feels her face blush at the thought of spending the night with Luca.

"Okay, my turn."

Kate sits up straight to show him she is ready to answer his question.

"What was the name of that book you mentioned, *Winks something*?"

"*When God Winks*."

"What is it about?"

"It's a collection of stories that show that what we call a coincidence, many people believe is God working to help us. So when something appears to be a coincidence, it is God winking at you, saying, 'I got this.'"

Luca ponders that for a moment. Then he looks at her, in her eyes, and asks, "Do you think God orchestrated our meeting, that we were destined to meet?"

So many thoughts race through Kate's head. Was she destined to meet Luca at this time and this point in her life? It's nice to think so. She feels so comfortable with him, and he pushes her. And he's an amazing dancer. And he's handsome and sexy. It's almost as if the universe heard her order for the perfect man and placed him in her path. She may have messed up London, but the universe has given her a second chance. She tries to reply to the question without revealing her true thoughts on the matter.

"I think everyone we meet is for a reason, sometimes to learn something, sometimes to teach something."

She realizes she didn't answer his question.

"Come on, Kate!" the voice in her head screams. "Tell him what you feel!"

"So, yes," she continues, "I think I do. There was something about you. I have a confession. I saw you downstairs at the club when you came in. I was drawn to you, and I saw you walking with such a purpose. And totally out of character for me, I decided to follow you."

"Aha!"

"Aha, nothing!"

"I just felt like saying that. If we are being honest, I saw you when you came into the room. You looked so lost, so out of place."

"That was a very good observation."

"Then I saw that guy ask you to dance. He had been asked to leave many times before, so I was going to come to stop you."

Kate just looks at him. He looks back at her.

Their moment is disturbed when the server comes up to the table, asking, "Anything else for you two?"

Kate shakes her head and takes the opportunity to fiddle with her napkin.

"No, I think we are good. I will take the check."

Kate starts to protest, but Luca reaches for it. "You have been through a lot today. It is the least I can do." He takes out his wallet and places a couple of bills over the check.

"Well, thanks for lunch, for saving me from drowning, for forcing me to take the plunge, for hearing me out, and for just being an all-around good guy." She feels silly after she says that last part, but it is true!

And apparently, it means a lot to Luca. "You think that? That I am an all-around good guy?"

"Absolutely!"

Luca beams the biggest smile, as if that was the first time anyone had told him.

Once the check is paid, he escorts Kate out of the restaurant. The square is alive with locals, and Kate is enamored with the lively buzz in the air. There are two older gentlemen playing chess outside a coffee shop. Mothers are shopping from the street vendors while their children run around.

Luca breaks the silence when he announces, "We have three hours until the ship sails." To which Kate responds, "Which means we have two hours until I want to be back on board before I get extremely nervous."

"Well then, let us adventure on!"

The remaining time is spent exploring the town. Luca and Kate become the ultimate tourists in this idyllic town, but at the same time seem to blend in quickly and look like locals. They take some pictures, smiling like a couple. Luca buys Kate a flower from the cart on the corner and tucks it in her hair behind her ear. They sample some fresh fruit. Kate returns a lost doll to a little girl. Luca plays a few quick soccer passes with a little boy. Kate watches as Luca moves through the small town with ease, looking relaxed and happy. Luca watches Kate do the same.

There's an ancient church in the town, the Great Cathedral, which becomes a must-visit for Kate. They find the cathedral, and Kate walks inside. She stops for a moment to feel the warmth and grace of the church. She walks over to the memorial candles and lights one, saying a prayer. Luca follows, and the two of them kneel at the side altar together. With heads still bowed, Luca reaches for Kate's hand. They leave the church hand in hand and head back toward the ship.

Once aboard, they part ways to their cabins to get ready for dinner. A comforting calm is shared by the two of them.

Luca bursts into his cabin and announces to Nikolai, "I am back! What a great day!" Not waiting for conversation, he heads into the bathroom and starts humming as he gets ready for the night.

Nikolai's interest is piqued. He wanders over toward the bathroom and pushes the door open. "Okay, what gives? I've never seen you like this. You're nice, helpful, happy. What's going on?"

Luca pokes his head out of the shower, "I am! One might even say I am an all-around good guy."

"Is the sex that good?" Nikolai asks.

Luca turns off the shower, wraps a towel around his waist, and comes out of the bathroom. "I would not know. We are only having fun together."

Nikolai scratches his head. "Now I am really confused."

Luca thinks for a moment before answering, "I am not sure I have an answer. I feel like a totally different person around her. We laugh; we talk about everything and anything. She has this calmness about her, but she gets flustered and excited. It is adorable. Everything about being with her is...easy."

"And she's got big knockers!" Nikolai reminds Luca.

"Yes, she does. Now let me get ready."

"You know you only have tonight and tomorrow and then back to London."

"I am well aware." There is no need for Nikolai to know that Luca promised to be a gentleman. Luca straightens his tie and turns to Nikolai. "How do I look?"

"Like a man on a mission." Nikolai's face softens, and he adds, "Hey, I am happy for you."

"Thanks. Do not wait up." And with that, Luca is out the door, headed to Kate's cabin.

Meanwhile, Kate is dressed and ready to go. She is standing in front of the mirror, scanning herself from head to toe, spinning around to admire her dress as it twirls. Gone is the self-doubt, the trepidation about what is to come. Kate is alive in the moment, soaking up every emotion. They are neither right nor wrong. They are what they are, and she is good with that.

Claudia returns to her cabin. She knocks on her friend's door to see how her day went, and is taken aback as the door flies open, revealing a beaming Kate.

"Wow, you look great!" she gasps. "Love the dress choice! Judging by that smile on your face, I would say you had a good day."

Unbeknownst to both women, Luca is approaching Kate's cabin. Since Claudia is standing in the doorway, he can hear the conversation between the two friends. A smile graces his handsome face as Kate's voice breaks through the cabin door and into his ears.

"It was absolutely amazing," he hears her say. "I never thought I would feel so alive again. I feel like with him, I can just be me."

Luca thinks the mission is accomplished. He's about to clear his throat to signal his arrival, but Kate is still talking.

"He kissed me at the beach! Oh, he is an amazing kisser! And you should see him with his shirt off! He's so strong!"

Luca loves to hear that.

Claudia scoffs and replies, "Just a kiss so far? He's taking this being a gentleman thing seriously, huh? You know you only have tonight and tomorrow, then back to London for our flight home."

"I know, that's why tonight after dinner I will make my move. Luca is going to break his promise about keeping his hands to himself. He just doesn't know it yet. I hear that dancers are really good at sex. They understand rhythm and all that."

Luca's smile fades as he contemplates Kate's words. He did promise to keep his hands to himself. Kate is changing all of that.

Claudia enters the cabin and closes the door behind her. Kate spritzes some perfume and asks Claudia, "How was your day?"

"I had a very nice afternoon. With everyone off in town, I had the ship to myself. Then I met Juan Carlos. He is one of the chefs. He took me on a tour of the kitchen."

"Fun!"

"He doesn't speak much English. But he made me the most delicious lunch and served himself for dessert."

"I don't know how you do it."

Outside, Luca feels it's not appropriate to linger and possibly hear more of this seemingly private conversation. Taking a deep breath, he steps closer, still not quite sure what to make of the new situation in which he finds himself.

Claudia smirks and teases Kate, knowing the soft knock on the door could only belong to Luca. "But you are about to find out," she teases.

Kate laughs and shushes her best friend as she walks toward the door. She opens it. Her breath catches as she looks at the devilishly handsome Luca.

"My lady," he says, "are you ready for a wonderful evening?" She looks beautiful, like an angel.

"More than you know." Oh, he knows alright.

Kate turns to Claudia and hugs her. "See you at dinner. We're going to stop by the lounge for a drink first."

Luca and Kate head down the hall toward the elevator. Kate feels some tension, an all too uncomfortable sensation that she has felt before. Luca stares straight ahead. Kate tries to get him to look at her, but he seems lost in another world.

"Everything okay?" she asks.

Her words seem to snap him back to earth. "Yes, I am sorry; I think I got too much sun today."

The elevator arrives. They walk in silently. Just before the door closes, Luca turns to Kate and says, "You look absolutely lovely."

"Thank you." Kate appreciates the compliment but still feels something is off in comparison to how their day went.

Entering the lounge, Kate is reminded of the fun she and Luca have had here and decides not to overthink Luca's distant mood. *Let's get this evening going with some conversation to set the stage*, she tells herself.

"What's your number-one sex fantasy?" she asks abruptly.

Luca almost chokes on his drink.

"Okay," he stammers. "Let us jump in with the sex talk. Usually, you preface it with 'I have a question.'"

"It's the new and improved jump-in Kate, thanks to you. So? What is it? Two women at the same time?"

"Did that already. It ranks up there." He winks at Kate. That always makes her smile.

"I forgot who I was talking to. Anything you haven't done?"

"I do not know about that. Are you asking for yourself or for the book?"

"Just making conversation." That's a white lie. She wants to start him thinking about sex—with her specifically.

"I see. What about you? What gets your panties moist?"

"That's an interesting choice of words. Well, it is probably pretty tame to you, but this is it." She reaches for her phone, starts scrolling through her pictures.

"Why am I not surprised that you have a picture of it?"

Kate shows him a picture of a man leaning into a woman who is backed up against a wall. The title is "A Proper Kiss." She mouths the words as he reads them aloud. "A proper kiss. Back her up against the wall. Use your knees to spread her thighs. Grab her wrists and

99

hold them one-handed above her head. Brush her hair from her face. Lift her chin until you meet her eyes. Look her intently in the eye as if you desire to devour her. Lean in closely. Wait for her to close her eyes. Then, and only then, brush your lips against hers. Let your tongue find hers. Never break the kiss first." Luca hands her back her phone.

Kate is flushed with excitement. "I added a twist: It happens in an elevator."

Luca doesn't seem to feel her excitement. "Very romantic. Why an elevator?"

Kate is taken aback by his lack of enthusiasm. He clearly doesn't see it as sexy as she does.

"Romantic? That's just hot! Sexy hot! *Steamy!* Something about an elevator, I don't know."

"I guess if that is what gets you going."

Kate is surprised by his response. She takes her phone back and puts it away. Luca gets up, holds a hand out for Kate.

"Ready for dinner?" He asks it like it is an obligation.

"Um, yeah, I'm starting to get hungry." Kate smiles weakly. She turns to head toward the door. That uncomfortable feeling returns and settles in her stomach.

Luca grabs her hand and spins her back around to face him. "I am sorry. That is the asshole I told you about. It is a very sexy fantasy. I can see why you like it."

His apology does not assure Kate; she still feels something is off, and she doesn't know why.

After a few drinks, Luca seems to relax and return to his usual playful self throughout dinner. He lets a slight touch linger, sending chills up and down Kate's body. He whispers in her ear, awakening her desire once again. He knows just how to look at her and smile that sexy smile that makes her weak in the knees.

They move to the ballroom, dancing the night away. Every time he holds her close, all she can think about is kissing him, wanting his hands and mouth all over her body and him inside her.

On the final dance of the night, he sends her back into a long dip. She remembers pushing her hips up into him and feels he has the same excitement growing. They burst out onto the deck, still warm and slightly sweaty from an evening of dancing. The cooler air is a welcome relief.

Kate is so ready to take the next step. She thinks he is ready too, and decides to just go for it. She leans in to kiss him, but he backs away.

"Um, it is getting late," he says. "I really think the day at the beach tired me out. I promised Nikolai that I would teach the class tomorrow morning, so I should probably take some time tonight to prepare for it." He knows it's a load of bullshit, but it's all he can think of on such short notice.

Kate clearly isn't buying it but tries to hide the hurt.

"Oh, um, yeah, of course. I wouldn't think you needed time...but, okay."

She takes a few steps back and begins to fidget with her dress. Luca realizes what he has just done but knows he can't go any further with Kate. What can he say to her? Should he tell her?

"Kate, I..."

Kate forces a yawn. "Oh wow, I didn't realize how late it was. Okay, well, good night." She turns to walk away, abruptly and fast on her heels.

"Kate!" Luca calls out to her.

She turns around. "Yeah?" she says with hope in her voice.

After an awkward moment of silence, all Luca can muster is "Goodnight."

Kate turns and hurries off, fighting back the tears as Luca watches her disappear inside. When she is out of sight, he punches the wall in frustration before heading back to his cabin.

EIGHT

The next morning, Luca finds himself knocking on Kate's cabin door.

"Come on, Kate, please open the door." Nothing. There is no sound inside. After a few moments, the door to the cabin next door is opened by a sleepy Claudia. She looks at Luca, who seems frantic.

"She's not in there," she says with a yawn. "And if she was, I don't think she would want to talk to you."

"She is mad?"

"She is hurt. I'm not sure what kind of game you're playing, but it's not nice." She wags a finger at him and begins to close the door, but Luca stops her.

"Can I talk to you for a moment, please?"

Claudia reluctantly opens the door wider and motions for Luca to come in. He comes in and crosses the cabin. Looking out the window over the water, he starts talking without turning around. "I am wondering, you know about our arrangement, yes?"

"Yes, she told me: sex and love discussions. Hands off, perfect gentleman. Yada, yada."

Luca turns to face Claudia. "I was to help her with certain parts of her book, yes, and she was helping me, well, let us say, understand love—and my problem in finding it."

"Okay," she says, growing impatient.

"I think I feel something I never felt before...with Kate."

Claudia sighs, raises an eyebrow, and stares at Luca. But Luca continues: "Being with her is so easy. She makes me laugh. She makes me think about things I have not thought about." This is all the truth, Luca reminds himself. "I know this sounds so strange, but as much as I wanted to, I couldn't. So I...well...backed up. I cannot explain it." He knows there is more to it, but this is all he can tell Claudia. "This is new for me. And I know she probably is really mad but I—"

Claudia holds up a hand to stop Luca. "One thing about Kate is she doesn't get mad...anymore," she observes. "I haven't seen her mad at anyone or anything for years. I think when her husband died, she experienced every feeling of anger she ever had or ever would have."

"I—" Luca attempts to interrupt.

"But you probably hurt her beyond imagination," Claudia forges ahead. "After her husband died, she had a very hard time opening up to anyone. You can't imagine what she went through. She couldn't let go, until you came along." Claudia gives Luca a very disappointed look, so much so that he backs up.

"Why am I afraid of you all of a sudden?"

Claudia laughs, mostly because she is glad that she got her point across. "She went to yoga this morning, so you might be able to find her there."

"Thanks." Luca sighs in relief.

Claudia makes a quick gesture that startles Luca. She smiles smugly as he takes notice and makes a point to walk around her as he heads for the door.

The ship's yoga studio is all windows on one side, overlooking the water and the magnificent views. There are perhaps twenty people taking the class. Everyone is pretty flexible, moving at their own pace. Kate has found a spot along the window, in the back. She needs some space to clear her head.

Luca peers through the window of the door and scans the crowd for Kate. He doesn't know exactly what he is going to say if she agrees to listen. But he knows she has the wrong idea, and he wants to make it right.

The instructor sees Luca at the door, opens it, and invites him in. He really just wants to get Kate's attention, but if this is the only way, he's willing to grab a mat and participate in the yoga class. He walks to the area where the mats are kept, searching for one. There's a momentary lull in the class as this intrusion interrupts the peacefulness of the group.

Kate turns to see what the commotion is, only to find Luca rummaging through a bin of mats. "Is he really coming to yoga?" she sighs to herself while deciding that the best reaction is no reaction. She returns her focus to her mat and tries to concentrate on her breathing.

Finally, Luca chooses a mat and takes off his shoes. He pads across the room to make his way to Kate. The room is crowded, and the participants are not happy with this late arrival. He knows Kate sees him, for there is a brief moment of eye contact, yet there isn't any other sign that she has acknowledged him. He drops his mat in between Kate and the person next to her, even though space is tight. The person gets up and moves his mat a few feet to give Luca enough room. Kate doesn't look up.

"*Scusi, scusi,*" Luca mutters, noticing the agitation caused by his disturbance.

"*Ciao,*" is all he can muster in Kate's direction. Knowing he has hurt her, which is too much to bear, he needs to make this right.

Kate mumbles a terse greeting in his direction but doesn't look at him. She is still embarrassed that her advances were rebuked the night before. She really doesn't think there is much he can say to explain. And she has convinced herself all morning that she really does not want to think about it any longer.

Luca is undeterred. When Kate rolls onto her back, he pops over almost on top of her. "Can I talk to you about last night, *per piacere*?" he pleads, hoping his Italian accent will win him some points.

Kate rolls onto her side then into a plank, almost knocking Luca off balance. Unwilling to give up, he squirms underneath her. "I know you are upset," he gasps, "and I want to explain."

A collective shush from the group sounds suddenly, making Kate tense.

"You can clear your conscience," she whispers. "I'm not upset." She moves to perform the downward dog position. Now her face is close to his. "So, if that was your desired outcome, I am sorry to disappoint you. You could just have told me that you didn't want to have sex with me. You didn't need to make up a lame excuse."

Even though she is whispering, the people closest to Kate and Luca are now intently listening to their conversation. One man, a few mats over, feels he needs to help.

"I'll have sex with you," he offers enthusiastically. He is promptly swatted by the woman next to him, presumably his wife.

Kate turns to Luca. "If you'll excuse me," she says firmly, "I'd like to finish the class in peace, without any interruptions."

Realizing he is not getting anywhere, he gets up to leave. "I am teaching the eleven o'clock class if you can stop by. I would really like to talk to you."

"Okay, I'll see," she replies, although she has already decided she has no intention of talking to him again.

Luca picks up his mat and tiptoes toward the door. A man on one side of Kate tells him, "Boy, are you in the doghouse!" Luca offers a pained grin and heads out.

A woman on the other side of Kate smacks her lips and says, "Honey, I don't know what he did, but I couldn't be mad at him!" Kate ignores the woman's words and goes back to her yoga. She takes a deep breath and chokes up as she smells Luca's cologne in the air. She fights back tears. Another deep breath.

Why did he have to come? she thinks, glancing at the door.

Claudia is waiting for Kate in the dining room, sitting at a nice table off in the corner. She's checking out the staff when Kate enters the dining room in a huff. Claudia sees her flustered friend and thinks, *Luca probably found Kate at yoga.*

Deciding to cut to the chase, and even though she already knows the answer, she asks, "How was yoga?"

"It was going fine," Kate says, "until Luca showed up wanting to explain about last night."

"So, what did he say?"

"He didn't get a chance. I told him there was nothing to explain. Everyone kept shushing him, so he asked me to come to the group class at eleven. Then he left."

"Okay, so not what I expected." Claudia tries to backpedal, but the look on Kate's face makes her confess. "Oh crap, sorry; I told him where he could find you. He was banging on your door, and I figured he wouldn't leave until he found you. You didn't want to hear him out?"

"Why, so he could *tell* me that he wasn't interested in having sex with me? Not exactly something I would enjoy hearing, especially how last night ended."

The server, who has just arrived, interrupts their conversation. "Good morning, can I get you something to drink?"

"I'll have a Bloody Mary."

Claudia is surprised at her friend's order and comments, "Why are you ordering that? You don't like Bloody Marys!"

Kate smiles and turns to the server. "She's right, I don't. I'll have a mimosa and an order of French toast." She's putting on a brave front, but Kate is rattled. The server straightens her place setting and returns to the kitchen.

"Thank you for that," Kate tells Claudia. "And before you say anything, I really don't want to talk about it anymore. I need to switch to Plan B. I've come too far, literally *too freakin' far* this time to chicken out like I usually do." Kate scans the room. "Who else can I turn my attention to tonight?"

Normally Claudia would try to stop her friend, but she can tell this is something Kate needs to do. But then again, no one compares to Luca. "One question: If you knew that it wasn't that Luca didn't want to have sex with you, would that change your mind to go talk to him?"

It's almost as if Kate doesn't hear her.

"Nope," she says, looking around the room. "Ah, here we go."

Claudia turns to see who Kate has selected.

"The captain?" she laughs. "Darling, he's—"

"Perfect! Distinguished gentleman, good, well, nice-looking. I'll be right back."

After Kate walks away, Claudia mutters, "I was going to say 'old,' but hey, what do I know?"

She watches as Kate nears the captain and begins talking to him. Kate laughs at something the captain says and then looks over at Claudia as the captain kisses her hand. They say their goodbyes before Kate walks away to rejoin Claudia.

"So, what was that all about?"

"Well, we are having dinner at the captain's table tonight, and I have a date for the grand ball afterward. I should have gone this route from the beginning." Kate seems pleased with herself, but Claudia can see through the charade to the pain her friend is feeling. Never one to let it show, Kate turns back to Claudia with a smile. "So, what do you want to do on our last day at sea? Ooh, I know! Spa treatments!"

Kate wolfs down the last of her French toast and gulps the rest of her mimosa. "Ready to bounce?"

"Yes, but I tell you what. Why don't you head over to the spa and get us all set up? I want to stop back at my cabin to get my book."

"You got it! I'll be waiting for you." Kate has an uncharacteristic spring in her step, which Claudia also recognizes as Kate not wanting to deal with her feelings. Claudia turns when Kate is out of sight and heads to the ballroom to find Luca.

She finds Luca wrapping up class, with an eye on the door, hoping Kate appears. He is excited for a moment when he sees Claudia but realizes she is alone. "She is not coming?"

"I'm afraid not. And she has lined up Plan B for tonight, if you know what I mean." Claudia winks, as horribly as Kate.

"What is it with you two not knowing how to wink? What is Plan B?"

"She got the captain to invite us to dine at his table tonight, then he is escorting her to the grand ball thingy. Look, I'm not sure why I am helping you, but fix this, will you? I know what she wants, even if she won't admit it."

"I will do my best. Thank you, Claudia."

Claudia returns to Kate at the spa, and the two are soon relaxing in the sauna after a massage.

"Kate, my dear, this was a good idea."

"Mmm, that's for sure." The soothing spa music and tranquil setting are helping Kate relax. Claudia, on the other hand, has thoughts swirling in her head.

"So, uh, I'd like to say one last thing about Luca," she says, "and I promise, not another word."

"Okay," Kate concedes. "Go ahead."

"I think you should hear what he has to say. I can't imagine that he didn't want to have sex. You were so cozy earlier in the day, and I saw how he was looking at you, so maybe there is a legit reason. And if that reason isn't really a bad thing, then I think he's a far better choice than the captain." Claudia realizes it's a convoluted argument, but none of this makes sense. She can see how much her friend is hurting and trying too hard to hide it and protect herself.

She has come so far—not necessarily in distance as Kate had thought, but emotionally—to give up now.

Kate contemplates her friend's words quietly. Claudia is glad to see her friend at least thinking about it.

"I thought it was a done deal, but he stopped. I mean, he put the brakes on! No matter what the reason, I feel like I would be pushing him into it, and I definitely don't want that. I would be so self-conscious. I want to be done feeling like that. You know that."

Claudia starts to object, but Kate cuts her off.

"I just don't think it was meant to be. We had plenty of chances and it didn't happen. And the one time I made a move? Rejected. I'm grateful for my time with him, no matter how it ended."

"I bet he would like to hear that from you," Claudia says, knowing she will appeal to her friend's sympathetic side.

"I suppose so. If I have the chance, I will tell him."

Kate and Claudia head out of the spa and back toward their cabins. Kate puts her arm around Claudia. "Thanks for coming with me. I never could have done this without you."

"Anytime, my friend."

⁓

For the last night of the cruise, the staff has arranged a very special dinner and black-tie party. This is the night when the women guests wear gowns and the gentlemen, tuxedos. It's a beautiful reminder of a time when string quartets played delightful dinner music while guests dined on a five-course meal. The party carries on into the ballroom, where a band plays music, champagne flows, and couples dance the night away.

Kate has looked forward to this night ever since she learned about the cruise. After spending the first few days with Luca, this last night was supposed to be the night of her dreams. She can picture Luca in his tuxedo. She even imagines him in tails and a top hat. She envisions walking into the ballroom on his arm, beaming from ear to ear when he asks her to dance, twirling around the dance floor, holding each other closely, ending the night with the most magical sex.

But here she is in her cabin, getting ready to put on her gown and head to dinner, knowing the rest of the night will not proceed how she had imagined. Dinner at the captain's table will be nice, as will being escorted to the dance on the captain's arm. But nice seems so boring now. Finally having her one-night stand doesn't seem as exciting as when she planned this trip. She knows what it's like to be in Luca's arms, and now she knows she will not end up in them. Is he going to be there? Should she talk to him? Maybe Claudia is right. Maybe she should hear him out. The more she thinks about it, she decides the best thing to do is get through this night, see what the captain is like, go home, and hope her time spent with Luca will have given her enough to rewrite her book. At least G will be happy she didn't have sex with a random stranger, although she isn't really sure why that bothered him so much.

She puts the finishing touches on her makeup, stares at her reflection in the mirror, and thinks about the kiss she shared with Luca yesterday at the beach. Seeing herself smile makes her realize it has been a long time since she has been as happy as she has been with Luca. The thought feels good, as does the thought that there are many more Lucas in the world, and that she will eventually cross paths with them. It's not the first time she has picked herself up and dusted herself off—and it probably won't be the last.

Luca is in his cabin getting ready for the evening, half-thinking he should just stay in and sneak off the boat as soon as possible tomorrow. As much as he wants to see Kate, to explain, to have one more night with her, he also knows he has hurt her. And that's the very last thing he wanted to do. Still, there's no way to explain things. It will only be worse, and he can't live with the idea of causing her any more pain. The best thing is to let her think he's a jerk and get on with her life.

As he stares at his reflection, his thoughts wander to the beach yesterday. Playing around with her in the water, seeing her blossom as she overcame her fear. He did that. He helped her feel safe and adventurous at the same time. At lunch, their conversation, hearing that she thought he was a good person. That came crashing down, didn't it? How on earth did it work out for them to meet like they did, to become friends like they did? What is that feeling he feels for her? It's new to him, but he likes it. He'll miss it. Maybe he'll find it again.

"Stop wallowing, Luca Bell'Angelo!" he scolds himself. He walks over to Nikolai's closet and pulls out the tuxedo with tails. He slicks his hair back. He has heard many times that he looks like a movie star when he dresses like this. He's going to need that star power tonight.

The dining room is transformed into another era. Kate's eyes widen and her jaw drops upon seeing the opulent decor, the men in tuxedos, the ladies in beautiful gowns. She and Claudia are escorted to the captain's table, where they are seated to each side of the captain, directly opposite each other. They exchange pleasantries with the other guests at the table, noticing the two seats directly to their sides are still empty.

The captain raises his glass to toast the guests. "I hope you all had a wonderful voyage, and that we will be seeing you on another adventure in the future!"

Everyone joins in a chorus of "Cheers!"

As Kate and Claudia begin the first course, a couple is escorted to the table and announced: "Mr. Luca Bell'Angelo and Mrs. Constance VanderHaven." Kate is startled to see Luca sit down next to Claudia and the woman next to her.

Forgetting where she is, Kate verbalizes a "Whoa" and fixes her eyes on Luca. Dressed in his tails, his hair slicked back, it seems the man has come straight from one of her dreams. Soon realizing that everyone is looking at her, her face flushes. Claudia and Luca know what prompted that outpour of emotion, but nonetheless she tries to cover with a lame excuse. "Claudia, look, there is chocolate lava cake for dessert! Whoa!"

She knows the statement has convinced no one, but it was worth a shot. Luca makes sure to look at her and smile his most devilishly handsome grin. He is satisfied that he got her attention. Constance decides to announce to the table, "I do apologize for being late. Luca is just the most amazing partner, and I didn't want to stop."

Luca rushes to add, "Dancing, of course."

Kate now is starting to get a picture of Luca cozying up to rich ladies on these cruises. She's not sure what his angle was with her. Perhaps he didn't think her money was worth the effort after all.

Kate decides to not give it another thought. What's done is done. She turns to the captain, touches his arm slightly, and starts a conversation about all the places he's been.

While Kate is busy chatting with the captain, Claudia says to Luca, keeping her eyes on Kate, "What are you doing?"

"Trying to get her attention."

"She doesn't like games."

"This is not a game, I promise."

The remainder of dinner is filled with great food, lots of drinks, and laughter. Kate does her best to avoid looking at Luca. Once the last dessert plate is cleared, Luca wastes no time in getting up. "Captain, lovely as always. My dear, shall we head to the ballroom?"

Kate lifts her head with a wanting look, but Luca is looking at Constance. Kate manages to keep it together as the two of them head out of the dining room. Once they have vanished from her sight, Kate is quick to turn to Claudia and raise an eyebrow as if to say, "What was that all about?" Claudia shrugs her shoulders.

Just then, an officer approaches the table to speak with the captain. He whispers something to him, then stands off to the side.

The captain addresses Claudia and Kate. "Ladies, I apologize, but there is something I need to tend to before the party. I don't want you to miss anything, so my chief officer, Charles, will escort you to the ballroom. I'll be there as soon as possible."

The final party is now in full swing. The orchestra is playing traditional ballroom music that fills the air as Kate and Claudia enter. Kate momentarily thinks about Luca when she sees all the couples dancing and twirling around the dance floor. The chief officer brings them to the captain's table, which is on the edge of the dance floor. Sitting where they are, it's impossible not to see Luca and Constance dancing.

Claudia notices Kate's expression. "Kate, dear, I'm not going to say anything else other than I want you to be happy, so do whatever makes you happy. But, good Lord, that man looks *hot*!"

"He does, doesn't he?"

"Will you be okay for a few minutes? I want to go make a request." Claudia rises, not really waiting for Kate to agree.

"Since when do you know any ballroom songs?"

"I have a salsa song I want to dance with that guy." Claudia waves at a handsome older gentleman on the other side of the dance floor and heads off toward the orchestra. Kate tries to look anywhere other than in the direction of Luca. The current song ends. Some couples exit the floor in search of a new partner, while other couples linger in place waiting for the next song to start. The bandleader is talking about something Kate can't quite make out. As she strains to hear, she sees Luca coming toward her, not taking his eyes off her. He stops in front of her, bows slightly and extends his hand.

"*Scusi*, Signora, may I have this dance?"

Kate opens her mouth to say something, but Luca quickly adds, "And remember, proper etiquette is to accept all dances." He winks and smiles a smile that melts her heart.

Kate looks up, returns the smile, and extends her hand toward his without saying a word. Luca leads her to the middle of the dance floor.

Time stands still for Kate as this moment is something from a dream—or from her deepest yearnings. Luca looks over at Claudia, nods, then turns his attention back to Kate.

Kate recognizes the beginning of the song "Time of My Life," one of her favorites. Luca lifts her chin until their eyes meet. "Time to put everything you learned together. Give it everything you got. You have this. I am here with you." It's like an angel speaking to her.

The melody takes over and Kate is consumed with it. From the moment she first heard the song, the words spoke to her.

> *I've been waiting for my dreams*
> *To turn into something*
> *I could believe in*
> *And looking for that magic rainbow*
> *On the horizon*
> *I couldn't see it until I let go*
> *Gave into love*
> *And watched all the bitterness burn*
> *Now I'm coming alive*
> *Body and soul*
> *And feeling my world start to turn*
> *And I'll taste every moment*
> *And live it out loud*

I know this is the time
This is the time
To be more than a name
Or a face in the crowd
I know this is the time
This is the time of my life.

Kate and Luca are moving as one around the floor, lost in the music, lost in each other. The other couples notice their sweeping movements and step aside as they move bigger and bigger. As the song comes to an end, Luca moves Kate into a super slow side dip, cradling Kate in his arms, her arms around his neck.

"You should do that more often. You are glowing," Luca proudly tells Kate.

"That was amazing. Thank you."

"My pleasure." Luca lifts Kate back to her feet but doesn't let her go. "Come with me."

Without hesitation Kate follows Luca out of the ballroom, holding hands. He stops and turns to face her. Luca looks Kate in the eyes and tells her, "I really need you to know something—"

Kate doesn't let Luca finish his sentence. She kisses him with such passion that when they come up for air, Luca holds Kate's face with an adoring look on his own. They stare into each other's eyes and smile an "I know where this is going" smile to each other. There's no need for words, only slight touches and caresses. Kate and Luca are glued to each other, not willing to let go.

The area of the deck where they find themselves is quiet, dark and secluded. Luca lifts Kate and backs her up against the wall. He leans in to kiss her but pauses for a moment. The pause only fuels their passion. They kiss deeper and deeper. He releases his hold on Kate, and she lands on her feet. With her still pressed against the wall, they resume kissing. His mouth travels to her exposed neck. He nibbles at the skin, sucking and licking just under her ears. Kate gasps as she feels Luca's hands touching her bare thigh under the skirt. He pulls down her panties as far as they can go.

"You are so beautiful," he breathes. "Oh, God, why did I deny myself?"

Luca removes his tuxedo jacket and loosens his tie. Kate starts to unbutton his shirt and progresses to unzip his pants. Luca backs up, steps out of his pants, and approaches Kate. He lifts her off the ground, out of her panties, and to the exact height that his rock-hard penis feels her wet arousal. Still holding her up with one arm, he guides himself slowly into her.

Kate is devoured by the intense passion. She eagerly accepts him. He fills her. The wild passion between them is still building. Luca lowers Kate until she is lying on her back atop his jacket. He's above her, inside her, moving in and out, causing deep moans to escape from Kate's mouth. Luca reaches behind Kate to unzip her dress enough to pull the top down below her shoulders, exposing her breasts. The light from the moon illuminates the lovers as they feel every aspect of each other's body. Luca thrusts until they both climax, then collapses on top of Kate. They stay this way for a moment before rolling onto their sides.

Once they catch their breath, they kiss once more and sigh, a sigh that signals the culmination of the intense passion that has been building since they met.

Luca helps Kate to a sitting position and realigns her dress. He put his pants and shirt back on, then leans against the wall with a deep breath. He turns and looks at Kate, only to find her gazing at him, taking a mental picture to always remember this moment. He notices she is biting her lower lip, her eyes bright.

"I guess I should have asked what to do in a moment like this," she says, proud of herself.

"I do not know, new one for me." He smiles that smile that makes her melt.

"Really?" she asks incredulously.

"Really," he repeats in a way that makes her believe him.

"So, now what?" Luca rises, extends a hand to help Kate up. He brushes the hair from her face and smooths it behind her ear. He brushes her cheek, smiles, and looks into her eyes. "We go dance some more, have a snack, and then more sex."

"I like snacks," Kate says with a wink—a proper wink that earns a nod of approval from Luca. They do their best to smooth out their slightly wrinkled clothes, and head back into the ballroom.

NINE

Morning arrives too fast for Kate. It seems as if her head has just hit the pillow when the day's first light begins to peek through the blinds. She ignores the natural urge to wake up and instead snuggles in the duvet for what seems like an hour or two until piercing tones of her phone's alarm awaken her. She looks at the time.

"Ugh, why can't I sleep in? What did I put on the alarm for?"

And then she remembers; today is the day when the ship docks from where they had started the cruise. The thought wakes her up completely. She slides out of bed and into the bathroom to prepare.

After some time, Kate and Claudia wait in the lounge with their suitcases. They have just finished their breakfast and are now waiting for the captain to give the call for departure from the ship. It's fairly early, so Kate yawns a few times.

Claudia grins at her friend, having heard the details of her night over breakfast. "I have a feeling you'll be sleeping on the plane. You sure you don't want to go say goodbye?"

Kate sits up straight and slaps the top of her thigh. "I'm sure. Last night couldn't have been any better. I'll leave it at that. I have more than enough material for my book, if you know what I mean."

A voice over the speaker calls their group. Kate and Claudia gather their belongings and head down the hallway that leads to the departure deck. Before heading through the door, Kate stops and turns to look back. Claudia notices this. "You *sure* you don't want to say goodbye? We have time."

"No, no; I was just taking one last look around." Kate turns back and heads off toward the walkway.

Claudia follows behind her, muttering, "Sure you were."

The taxi ride to the airport is not very long. Kate is leaning her head against the window, not into seeing the sights like she was the day they arrived.

Claudia uses this opportunity to interrogate her about the happenings of last night.

"So, how did you leave it with him?"

"He woke up around 5:30, got dressed, kissed me goodbye, and said something in Italian I didn't quite get. I heard the word *spiacente*—means "sorry"—and some other words. I was too exhausted to ask. We didn't really decide on anything. It was odd for me; I didn't want to get all wrapped up in making plans. I was going with the flow, and it was a nice feeling. We joked that I would smuggle him home in my suitcase. I'm not sure what either of us expected, but the last few hours were heavenly."

"Would you want to see him again?"

"Oh, my gosh, yes!"

"So no plans to meet again?"

"We kinda talked about maybe him coming to New York sometime or me meeting him in London, or maybe another cruise, but nothing concrete. He has my number; I have his. I don't know what to think. I wanted one night of passion, and I got that and so much more. I mean, that's what was in his mind, I think. I just don't know what to think, you know? I know I am not making any sense."

"Wow, he really got to you, huh? Don't get me wrong, that's a good thing. I like the changes I see. Mostly that huge smile on your face." She pats her friend on her arm.

"Thanks. I definitely got more than I thought from this trip. I feel like I have some clarity about what was holding me back, and how to move forward." Kate returns to looking out the window as the taxi approaches the airport.

After checking in, Kate and Claudia look for comfortable seats near the gate to wait for the time to board. To pass the time, Claudia begins watching a Broadway show on her laptop, while Kate catches up on her missed text messages.

There's a text message from G. "Okay, that's odd. G offered to pick us up at the airport. Okay with you?"

Claudia looks at her, grins, and says, "Oh, yes, that would be lovely."

She goes back to her movie while Katie ponders the unexpected offer from G. "Wonder what got into him?"

An announcement calls for first-class boarding. Kate and Claudia get up and head toward the door.

Claudia signals for Kate to go ahead. "After you, dahling! Back to the real world."

"Yup."

Kate looks back once before handing her boarding pass to the attendant.

"Fond memories of the airport?" Claudia teases her friend as they head down the jetway.

Kate laughs loudly. "Haha! Okay, so maybe I was thinking that he'd come running down to the gate with minutes to spare before I get on the plane." Kate holds up her hand in anticipation of what she knows Claudia will say. "I know, I know; not the movies."

"Yes, and if he did do that, he'd probably have Security chasing after him."

At the airplane door, the ladies turn to the left to find their seats. Claudia continues, "Although I guess it would be fun to experience a movie moment like that." Kate doesn't answer but asks, "Can I have the window?"

"Sure. We're row 4, on that side." Claudia points to the right.

"Are you sure? There looks to be someone already there."

"That's the seat. If it's a cute guy, find some other place to sit, okay?"

Looking over her shoulder at Claudia, Kate jokes, "Wow, you'd leave me just like that—" Kate doesn't finish her sentence because as she arrives at row 4, she sees Luca sitting in her seat.

"Surprise!" Claudia yells, although she's certain her friend does not hear her.

Luca starts to speak. "I hope you do not mind that I—" Before he can finish, Kate drops her bags, jumps into Luca's lap, and kisses him. Claudia picks up Kate's things and takes her seat across the aisle from the love connection that is still happening.

Claudia mutters to herself, "I don't think she minds."

When Kate comes up for air, she looks over at Claudia. "You knew about this?" Claudia flashes a cheesy smile. Kate then turns her attention back to Luca. "How did you get on the plane ahead of us?"

"Your friend is quite the carnivore."

"Conniver," Kate corrects. "And yes, she is! She is quite proud of that."

"This one ranks up there." Claudia pats herself on the back. "Now you two go back to what you were doing."

Kate is still sitting on Luca's lap. "Oh, my goodness, just like in the movies. How did you plan this?"

Luca takes advantage of the close proximity to Kate and begins to play with her hair. "After I left you this morning, I woke up Claudia to get your flight information."

"Lucky for you there was a first-class ticket left. I don't do coach," Claudia chimed in.

Kate laughs knowingly and beams at her friend. "Thank you for knowing what I want, even when I don't."

"That 'sick puppy' look this morning was killing me. I wanted to tell you so badly."

Claudia starts to laugh at the mental image, thinking back to the hours leading up to this moment. The laughter becomes hysterical.

"What's so funny?"

"I just thought about the added bonus. I'll get to see G's face when you walk off the plane with Luca. Please let me get a picture of that!"

"G's not going to care."

Claudia scoffs at her friend and says, "I wouldn't be so sure about that."

⌒

G is standing at the window of his Manhattan office, looking out over the city. His assistant walks in and clears his throat to get his boss's attention. G turns around. He is expecting an update.

"All set?" he asks.

"Yes, reservations are set for Il Tulipano at eight, your favorite booth. The limo will pick you up downstairs, head to the airport, then on to the restaurant."

"Perfect. Can you make sure there are flowers and champagne in the limo?"

"Roses?"

G chuckles. "Not roses. Lots of colorful flowers, all types."

"Must be someone special you're picking up. Anyone I know?"

"As a matter of fact, you know her very well. Kate Covington."

"Oh," the assistant intones. Then he cocks his head, looks at G, and follows with, "*Oh!* Finally!"

"Yes, I know, takes me a little longer. These past few days, with her gone, I realize I have feelings for her. I want to tell her, and I want the mood to be just right. She's coming back from a cruise, so we'll drop her friend off and then go on to dinner."

G leaves for the airport and arrives just before the plane lands. He waits nervously for Kate and Claudia to emerge at the baggage claim area of JFK. He's pacing back and forth, looking up every time someone comes through the door. Finally, he sees Kate and smiles.

She looks good, tanned and relaxed, he thinks. *Something is different.* G cannot quite figure out what seems different about Kate, but all he cares about now is that she is back and he is happy to see her.

Kate spots G from a distance and runs up to him, drops her bags, and wraps her arms around him. He gives her his customary squeeze then, out of character, kisses her on the lips.

"Welcome home, Claudia. Nice to see you," he says, but all he can think about is getting rid of her as fast as possible.

"Oh, yes, it is. Thanks so much for coming to get us."

"Wait, you're happy to see me? You ladies must have been drinking on the plane,"

"Yes, we were, and we should have brought you one."

Kate is quick to quash that conversation. "Don't mind her. I have some news."

"You brought home an old dog?"

Claudia is quick to interject, "More like a puppy."

Kate gives her friend the you're-not-helping-me look.

"It's actually pretty funny. You'll get a kick out of this. You know how all the times you would travel, and I would tell you to bring me back a hot young guy?"

"Yeah?" G has a bad feeling. He doesn't like where this is going.

"Well, I brought home my own hot young guy." She flashes a cheesy smile.

"You *what*?"

At that moment, Luca strolls up, puts his arm around Kate, and extends his right hand to G. "You must be G. I hear a lot about you. I am Luca."

G shakes his hand, ignoring Claudia's intent gaze, which swings between him and Luca as if she's following a tennis match. "Um, well, can't say the same, but, um, well a friend of Kate's is well, um, well... welcome to New York."

G never stammers or searches for words. Luca breaks the silence. "Ladies, show me which bags are yours."

Luca heads over to the baggage carousel. Claudia follows, as does Kate until G grabs her arm and stops her in her tracks.

G is beside himself. "Now I know you have lost your mind. What on earth are you thinking bringing him back with you?"

"What?" Kate is taken aback by G's tone. "Aren't you the one that is always telling me to live a little?"

"A little, Kate! This is not a little. This is a lot, bringing some random guy you met on a cruise home with you."

"Actually, he worked it out with Claudia to get a plane ticket on our flight, but that's beside the point. I am thrilled! Give me some credit, though. I know everything about him. He's a professional ballroom dancer."

"Oh, well, okay then. That's good to know," G says sarcastically. He has his hands on his head now. "Seriously, I can't even—" G turns away from Kate.

She runs right around to face him. "We spent just about the whole cruise together. I know all I need to know about him."

G just huffs and stares at her. "You can't possibly know everything about him after five days."

"Really, I don't understand why you are so mad. You're acting like I just ruined your day." G says nothing. He just looks at Kate. "If you give him a chance, you'll like him too, okay?"

G doesn't have a chance to answer as Luca and Claudia return with all the luggage. Kate tries to smile through, unnerved a bit by G's reaction. "Oh, I almost forgot, I brought you a present!"

"A Swedish stewardess, I hope."

"Now that's the G I know. I got you a bottle of that brandy you really like." And then she's off to catch up with Luca.

"Hope it's a big bottle," G mutters as he follows them out of the airport.

Once outside, G takes the lead and heads toward the limo. Claudia sees the driver approach them to handle the luggage.

"Nice going, G." She pokes her head in the limo through the open door. "Flowers, champagne; are we crashing a date or something?" Claudia senses what he is up to.

"What can I say? This limo company goes all out for its customers." G pours the champagne and hands everyone a glass. "Celebrating a new author!"

"Thanks, G." Kate blushes as she sips her glass of bubbly. "These flowers are absolutely beautiful. My favorite!"

G looks at her, about to say something, then stops himself. He smiles stiffly and silently wishes the limo ride to be over as soon as possible. "Claudia, where can we drop you off?"

"My car is at Kate's."

"Okay, good. Luca, what hotel are you staying at?"

Claudia coughs and tries to stifle a smile. She enjoys seeing G squirm a bit.

"He's staying with me of course," Kate volunteers as she squeezes his arm.

"Of course." G pours more champagne. He attempts to make some conversation to cover the awkward silence.

"So, Luca, first time to New York?"

"I have been to the city a few times, but first time to Lawn Guy Land. How did I do?" He turns to Kate for approval of his New York accent.

"Mahvelous!" She and Luca kiss and giggle. G wants to vomit.

"How long are you staying?"

"I have my return to London on the 25th."

"That's too bad. That's the night of my birthday party. You could have come with Kate. Best Italian food—you would think you're in Italy."

Kate touches Luca's arm. "Wait, I thought you left on the 26th?"

"Yes, you are right. Not a lot of sleep last night," he answers, causing Kate to blush.

Claudia waits for her chance to say, "Look at that, G. He can make it after all. Isn't that great?"

If looks could kill, Claudia would be dead on the floor of the limo. "That's swell," G mutters as he turns his attention to the road signs. He's counting the exits until they arrive at Kate's.

The limo driver helps unload all their luggage and puts Claudia's in her car. Claudia hugs Kate and waves to Luca and G before she drives off. Meanwhile, Kate walks to her front door and opens it. She heads inside, followed by Luca and G. They are met by the thunderous sound of barks and paws pounding on the wooden floor.

They jump and yip in excitement, which is their version of saying, "Hello! Welcome home! We are so happy to have you back. We missed you very much!" After this, they immediately swarm around Luca.

"Awww *cani*!" he cries. "Hello, puppies!" He pets them lovingly. They look at G, who makes a face at them. They turn away to follow Kate into the kitchen.

Kate's voice comes from the kitchen. "Guys, make yourselves at home. I'm fixing their dinner. I think Chelsea has already left to go back to the dorm."

Luca looks around the living room and asks G, "Will you point to me the way to the restroom?"

G looks up from his phone and points, "Down the hall, to the left. *Non mi piace che tu sia qui.*"

Luca looks at G but says nothing. He disappears down the hall just as Kate comes back into the room.

"What don't you like here?"

G is surprised that she understood part of what he said in Italian. "When did you start speaking Italian? I don't like this chair here." He isn't about to tell her that he doesn't like Luca being here, even though he really wants to.

Kate looks puzzled. "It's been there forever. And I just started, for obvious reasons." She sits down in the chair, sighs, and tells G, "Thanks for picking me—us—up. It's good to be home."

"I'm guessing you have ample material for your book, so I will expect a revision on my desk in a week."

"Make it two," she says with a smile. "You want a drink?"

"As much as I'd love to be an extremely awkward third wheel, no, thanks. I have to go. I have dinner plans."

"Ooh, where ya going?"

"Tulipano."

"Fancy schmancy. Who are you trying to impress?"

"Nobody. Just a client. An attorney's work is never done."

Kate gets up to walk G to the door. "Make sure you are ready to negotiate a lucrative book deal. I have a good feeling about this." She smiles at him, gives him a hug and a kiss on the cheek. "Talk to you tomorrow."

"You got it, missy."

Kate closes the door behind him, leans against it, and sighs. She never imagined she could feel this good again.

Luca comes back into the room. "I thought it got quiet out here."

"Yes, nice and quiet. I loved the cruise, but I'm not used to being around so many people at once."

Luca walks toward Kate, his eyes fixed on her. "Yes, I think I am going to like just me and you for a while." He stares at her face for a few seconds before leaning in to kiss her neck.

"Are you hungry?" Kate interrupts. "I can make you something."

"Nope." He moves to the other side of her neck.

"Thirsty?"

"Nope."

"Are you sure?"

To stop Kate from asking any more questions, Luca kisses her on the mouth, probing with his tongue. They kiss for some time, just enjoying the feel of each other's bodies. After a while, Kate becomes impatient and starts to unbutton his shirt. She slides it off and caresses his shoulders, back, arms—anywhere her hands can touch, as long as it's Luca's warm skin.

Meanwhile, Luca makes his own path. He reaches around and unzips her dress, which then falls to the ground. With his hands on her waist, he pulls her closer as they kiss even deeper. Luca loses control briefly when Kate takes his lip in between hers and sucks lightly. She tugs the lip, then licks it with her tongue.

Luca picks Kate up, walks to the couch, and lays her down. He stands to his full height while staring at the woman laying before him, her eyes looking up at him as if she would prefer nothing but to eat him alive. He unzips his pants and steps out of them. He lays his naked body on top of her and begins touching and exploring every inch of her smooth body, touching the side of her breasts and her thighs, all while sucking on her neck. Within moments, Kate begins to squirm and runs her hands along his back. She sits up, still kissing and caressing. Then she stands up and, without taking her eyes off of Luca, removes her bra and slips out of her panties. Luca gulps, not able to take his eyes off the woman.

She moves toward him and straddles him, taking his hard, erect penis into her with ease. He moans. She moans. As she moves up and down, the passion intensifies until she throws her head back and screams with delight.

TEN

The morning after that glorious night, Kate is in her kitchen, preparing a breakfast feast for Luca. Wearing only a loosely tied silky robe, she hums along to the music in her head, engrossed in reliving memories of the night while also trying to focus on making breakfast. She doesn't realize Luca has come downstairs. He stands just outside of the open kitchen and smiles at seeing her so happy, dancing in place in front of the stove.

Just as she is about to flip a pancake, he says with a chuckle, "This is a new way to turn on a stove."

Kate jumps in surprise, the pancake launching across the room toward Luca. "Ah, sorry, not used to having people around. Sleep okay?"

Luca retrieves the errant pancake and brings it to the counter by Kate. "I did, indeed. You?" he asks as he wraps his arms around her from behind.

"I did. Hungry?"

"Famished!"

"Breakfast is almost ready. Do you want coffee?" Kate points to the full pot on the counter.

"Sure." Luca pours a cup and stops to look at the things on Kate's refrigerator. There are various photos and a calendar with today's date circled, held in place by magnets. He stops at the photo of a young lady who looks very much like Kate. "Is this your daughter?"

"Yes," Kate smiles. "That's Chelsea."

"*Che bella.*"

"She is beautiful. Inside and out, and creative and fierce! Not like me. She takes after her dad."

"I think that is exactly you." Luca looks at the calendar. "Is this calendar for your dance studio?"

Kate was hoping he would see that, but now she is suddenly shy. "Oh, yeah, um, yes, that's it...I think." Trying to play coy is not a personal strength. She bites her lip and brings a big platter of breakfast items to the table.

"There is a party tonight?"

"Oh, maybe, I think so. Not that I can remember."

"Hmm..." Luca looks intently at the woman in front of him who doesn't meet his eyes. Looking to change the subject, Luca admires the food on the table. He's impressed with the breakfast selections, secretly delighted that Kate cooked for him. It's been a long time since someone has fussed over him like this.

"Wow, this all looks amazing!" He proceeds to fill up two plates, giving one to Kate. "Do you want to go?" he asks innocently while taking a bite of the pancakes doused in syrup.

"Go where?"

"You should not play poker," Luca laughs. "Your face will give you away every time! Go to the party...that's if you *want* to go."

"Well, I was thinking maybe we could stop by, you know, if there's time."

Luca is grinning now. "Hey, I get it. You want to show me off. I am quite a catch. 'Arm candy' is the expression, I believe." He flexes his bicep and folds his one arm to prove his point.

Kate laughs and replies, "Yes, that is, and yes, you are."

Feeling pleased with himself, Luca launches into what they could do later that night.

"Okay, here is the plan. Pick your favorite place for dinner, put on your favorite dress, and we will arrive to the party twenty minutes after it starts. That should make for a nice entrance, do you not think so?"

Kate gives him an inquisitive look.

Luca raises one eyebrow. "Do not look at me like that. I have been around ballroom dancing since I was a child. I know how you ladies think. And I would be right to guess that there is one person in particular you will be happy to, how you say, 'stick it to.'"

Kate tries to feign outrage, but she knows Luca won't buy it. "I am not that type of person! Oh, who am I kidding? Amanda Pearson—ooh, she gets under my skin."

"I thought so."

The two finish their meal chatting away.

Wiping his hands on a napkin, Luca says, "Now run along and get dressed; I will clean up."

Kate looks at him with that same inquisitive look.

"Yes, I help with the dishes. So go before I change my mind."

Kate smiles, drops her napkin, and springs from her chair. "Okay, I'm outta here." She kisses him, and he smacks her ass.

Upstairs in her bathroom, Kate is back to humming while she undresses and gets in the shower. As the water cascades over her, she exhales and closes her eyes, a small smile curling the corners of her mouth. She spends a little more time than usual in the shower, imagining the night ahead of them and thinking again of the night they spent in each other's arms. Afterward, she moisturizes, spritzes, and primps her body and hair, leaving no inch of skin unattended.

Thinking about what to wear, she remembers a lace lingerie set in the back of a drawer. She crosses the bedroom and stops in front of the dresser. On top is a wedding picture of her and Peter. In a swift move, she puts the picture in a drawer as she retrieves her undergarments and heads back to the bathroom. On second thought, she heads back to the dresser, retrieves the picture, and returns it to its spot. Moving on doesn't have to mean forgetting.

Meanwhile, Luca is busy tidying up the kitchen. Once done, he looks around the home, marveling at what he sees. He couldn't have imagined how warm he feels standing inside Kate's little world. Being here tells Luca so much about the woman who had taken his breath away with the first glance.

Her pantry and fridge are arranged neatly. She has tons of photos of her daughter and her dogs. Her knickknacks all express some form of love, faith, hope, or perseverance. He comes across her bookshelf, peruses the titles until he sees *When God Winks*, and pulls it off the shelf. He drops it on her big, oversized chair, planning to read it later, then heads upstairs to find her.

Once inside her room, he can hear her humming from the bathroom. There is a little alcove on the side of the room with a bench seat under a window. On top of one of the pillows, he finds a scrapbook labeled "Keep Moving Forward." Still curious to learn all he can about Kate, he flips through the pages to find a collection of motivational quotes and photos.

"One day you will tell your story of how you've overcome what you are going through now, and it will become part of someone else's survival guide."

Another one, in bold white letters on a black background: "The Universe said I need you to get excited again. I need you to remember you are not in this thing alone. I'm working on your challenges; I've already assigned angels to you. So let go of the stress and just trust Me; I've got a pretty incredible ending in store. In fact, that's why you need to get excited again...because the happy ending I've got coming, is going to ROCK. YOUR. WORLD."

Kate emerges from the bathroom and sees him looking in her scrapbook. "You helped me take that most important next step," she says.

"*Scusi?*"

"I've collected all of these sayings over the past few years. All of them have spoken to me on some level to let me know that one day I would fall back together again. Meeting you helped me take that next step, which was to stop fighting and let it happen."

Luca doesn't know what to say; he's not used to being on the receiving end of such a genuine compliment. This is a life-altering moment for him. He bows his head in honor of its significance but, unsure how to respond, deflects the conversation to the dance party.

"I am happy to have helped. So, let me see this stunning dress you are wearing tonight." He heads for her closet as she happily follows behind.

The Ballroom Dance Studio is considered one of the best places on Long Island for ballroom dancing. Fortunately for Kate, it is located in the town where she lives. The building features a large, beautiful studio with white billowy curtains draped from the ceiling, crystal chandeliers, and decorations reminiscent of ballroom dancing through the ages. Max, one of the owners, has been Kate's teacher from the time she and Peter first started taking lessons. He is an amazing dancer, and he and Kate clicked from day one.

Their Saturday-night parties are always a big draw, with most of the students dressing up to practice and socialize with the other dancers. Kate can tell that tonight is no exception; the parking lot is packed. She can see figures dancing inside and is excited to dance with Luca in this environment.

Luca can tell her mind is a million miles away. "What are you thinking?"

"I am realizing that I am very excited to introduce you to Max and to dance with you, when, under other circumstances, I think I would have been afraid to go in. I don't come very often since Peter died. It can be awkward. But now..." Her eyes light up with excitement. "Now," she purrs as she leans over to kiss him, "I am walking in with the most handsome, sweetest, dance stud of a man."

Luca looks at her fondly. "I am glad to see you so happy."

"I smell a 'but.'"

"*Scusi?*"

"It sounds like you are going to say 'but...' and then something else."

Thinking for a second, and realizing she is right, he smiles.

"Yes, *but* I think you need to give yourself more credit. I am not responsible for this change. You were ready. I just happened to be at the right place at the right time."

"I appreciate the compliment, at least I think that was a compliment, *but* I don't think you give yourself enough credit for my transformation. You knew what I needed and when I needed it. It's like you knew me before you met me."

Something about what Kate says makes Luca slightly uncomfortable. Determined to make sure she has the most wonderful experience tonight, he snaps out of it. "Well, we are two amazing people. That is what it is. *Andiamo*! I want to show you off!"

Inside the ballroom, the party is in high gear. Couples are dancing; people are mingling by the bar, scouting their next dance partner. Max is finishing a snack while Amanda tries her very best to flirt with him. Not getting anywhere again this time, she tugs on his arm to get him to dance with her as the next song is about to start. They are dancing when Kate and Luca walk in, stop at the reception area, and say hello to Janelle, the receptionist.

While they catch up, Max notices Kate.

"Hey, Kate's here!" he says, happy to see her. Amanda is less impressed; this means fewer dances—and less attention—for her.

As they move around the dance floor, Amanda now sees Kate at the door. "And it looks like she has a date." Now Amanda is happier—more men to ask her to dance.

After Amanda's proclamation, it's Max's turn to be in line to see the door. "Holy shit! I think that's Luca Bell'Angelo!"

Amanda hears the excitement in Max's voice and turns to look herself. "You mean ballroom dancer Luca Bell'Angelo? Ten dance champion Luca Bell'Angelo?"

"It sure looks like him."

"What the hell?" Amanda can take it no more and uncouples from Max to head to the door. "Kate, dear, so lovely to see you!" she says loudly from across the floor. The woman, dressed all in red, with silky chestnut hair tumbling down her back in waves, approaches the couple.

Seeing the woman, Luca whispers in Kate's ear, "Let me guess; that is Amanda."

"What gave it away?"

"Every studio has one. They are all the same."

Amanda is standing right in front of them now. She's talking to Kate but can't keep her eyes off Luca. "Kate, it's been forever! How are you? And *who* is this?" She's not even trying to pretend any interest in Kate at this point. "Hello. I'm Amanda Pearson," she says as if Luca should know the name, brushing past Kate to introduce herself to the man.

"Luca Bell'Angelo." He shakes her hand.

Kate is already tired of Amanda. "And this is Max, the fabulous dancer who taught me everything I know." Kate gets in between Luca and Amanda to usher him closer to Max.

"Pleasure to meet you, Luca. Welcome!"

"Thank you, very nice to meet you. Kate says wonderful things about you. You have taught her well."

Amanda tries to wiggle into the conversation. "I'm one of Max's students—"

"Ah!" Luca interrupts, now doing his part. "I love this song! Excuse us. Shall we, my dear?"

Kate knows what he is up to, and it makes her happy. "I would love to."

They walk out onto the floor, leaving Max smiling, Amanda stunned, and everyone else wondering, "Who is this handsome man who won't take his eyes off Kate?"

All eyes are on them as they stand in frame for a minute, swaying to the music.

"Everyone is like, 'What the heck?'" Kate observes.

"That mouth of yours!" Luca feigns his displeasure. He has to laugh at that comment. He realizes, too, that there isn't a single thing about Kate he would change. "Let us give them something to look at then, yes?"

"My thought exactly." Kate winks at him.

"I was hoping you would say that," he says, winking back.

Kate and Luca dance around the floor as if there is no one else in the room. One by one, they take bigger strides, more swooping movements, until finally there isn't a person in the room not watching them. When they finish, everyone erupts in applause. Luca is proud. He spins Kate out to take a bow.

Reluctant at first, she obliges after a simple smile and nod from Luca. He is proud of his student. Kate glows from the praise and applause. They walk back to where Max is standing. By now, word has circulated among the crowd exactly who Luca is, and everyone clamors to meet him.

Kate sits off to the side to avoid the crowd. She adjusts her shoe. Her thoughts turn to Peter, and one day in particular. Kate remembers that day like it was yesterday. It was a Friday night, and Peter had come home from work looking rather sad. He had been struggling with life and its many worries and growing increasingly unhappy. Kate asked him what was wrong. She wasn't prepared for the answer. He told her that he had been thinking about ending his life. That night there were a lot of tears, a lot of upset.

The next morning, he seemed a lot happier. He told her not to pay attention to what he said the night before. She felt better after hearing this, but there was always a nagging doubt in the back of her mind that Peter wasn't being truthful.

Kate comes back to the present, feeling as if Peter is sitting next to her on the bench. Looking sideways, she sees him smiling fondly at her. She hears his voice: "I'm glad he likes to dance."

There is momentary silence as the sounds of the ballroom are muted. Then, suddenly, noise erupts, breaking off the conversation Kate was sharing with her beloved dead husband. There is so much she wants to talk to him about, but at this moment she feels a wave of peace wash over her.

Max walks over to her and extends a hand. "This rumba has your name on it. May I?"

Kate offers a smile, stands up, and accepts his hand. She always loves dancing with Max. He is pleasantly surprised that she has become such a confident dancer. "I always knew you had it in you."

"Really?"

"You just had to let it out. I'm happy for you."

"Thank you. I'm happy for me too."

"Okay, I have to know. How did he get you to open up?"

Kate thinks for a moment. "I'm not sure it was one specific thing. He pushed me, that's for sure, and I always felt secure with him. He let me be me."

Max smiles. Then Kate adds, "And the sex certainly helped!"

They both laugh and continue enjoying the dance.

ELEVEN

Early in the morning five days later, Kate is sitting at her computer, typing away. Luca comes into the room and notices a slight smile on her face.

"How is it that you always get up so much earlier than I do?" He kisses her and strokes her hair. "And you fall asleep so fast! I have never seen a woman just roll over and fall asleep like you."

"Just lucky, I guess," she says as she shrugs her shoulders.

Standing behind her still, he runs his hands through her hair again, knowing how much she enjoys it. He rubs her neck, slowly moving his hands down toward her breasts. He caresses them over her shirt, taking his time before making his way inside and pinching her nipples ever so slightly. He can tell she is getting aroused as she abandons her typing and moans softly. He intensifies his touch, grabs both breasts harder, tugs on her now fully erect nipples. He lowers his head to find her mouth, licking at her lips before parting them with his tongue, all while still fondling her breasts. Kate moans with delight. Luca slowly moves one hand lower, slipping into her lace panties to find her dripping wet with desire. Leaving his mouth close to hers, barely touching hers, he makes one sweeping movement of his hand to which Kate responds with a loud groan.

"Holy moly!" she exhales. "I think I saw stars."

"Happy to lend a hand." He winks and backs away.

She watches him pour a cup of coffee and shakes her head, still not able to believe this isn't a dream. After that orgasm, she is too distracted to return to her writing. "So, what do you want to do on your last day here?" She walks over to him and runs her hands up his chest. "Change your flight and stay a little longer?"

He stops her hands from going further. "I think it is for the best that I go back home and let you write."

Kate makes a sad face. She knows she isn't writing as much as she should. "I guess. And we still have tonight. You will love this restaurant. Best Italian food!"

"I do not think G is too excited that I am coming."

"Oh, don't be silly. He loves having people around."

Looking to change the subject, Luca tells Kate, "After you fell asleep last night, I started thinking."

"A-n-n-n-d…" Kate draws out the word, unsure where Luca is going with his thought.

"What do you say we meet in Vienna for New Year's Eve? I have friends there we can stay with; the winter is just beautiful and, of course, New Year's Eve is the start of the ball season."

"That sounds absolutely awesome. Only one problem: I don't think I can wait that long to see you again."

"We will have to make the most of tonight then. Get your fill, as they say." He smiles mischievously. "And we can always Skype or FaceTime. Do you have a vibrator?"

Kate blushes, but this time she welcomes the tingling. She knows her senses are coming alive again.

"No?" he prompts.

"I might," she stammers, "tucked away somewhere." Desperate to change the subject, she looks down at her watch theatrically and exclaims, "Oh, wow! Look at the time! I have a hair appointment. I'll be back in about two hours. Make yourself at home."

She kisses him goodbye—a nice, lingering kiss.

"See you later." And she is out the door.

Luca settles into the comfy living room chair with both dogs and opens *When God Winks*. Once he starts reading, he can't put the book down. Not only is the material incredibly interesting, but everything inside the book is so relatable. He thinks over many events in his life in which he now knows God was by his side, even if it didn't seem like it at the time. Turning to his present situation, he thinks about how Kate was brought into his life. Was it fate that led the two to meet in London before they met on the cruise? Whatever it was—chance, coincidence, or something else—he's glad the universe is conspiring for him when it comes to the woman who has bewitched him soul, heart, and body.

G's birthday is held every year at Il Tulipano, a traditional Italian restaurant run by an Italian family. You would think you are sitting at a restaurant in Italy, because everything—from the decor to the ambience to the food—is authentic. The private dining room is already full with thirty people when Kate and Luca arrive. G is sitting next to a woman Kate doesn't recognize. They are ushered to two empty seats by a staff member, who welcomes her as if she is a member of the family.

"Hi, everyone!" Kate announces. "This is Luca!" Luca waves in acknowledgment.

"Hi, Kate; Hi, Luca."

"Happy birthday, G!"

G rises. He and Kate give each other a long hug and kiss on the cheek before he turns to his companion. "Sydney, this is Kate and her...Luca. Kate, this is Sydney."

Kate puts on her nice voice. "Hi, Sydney. So nice to meet you." Luca shakes her hand and says a quick hello. They take their seats.

Kate whispers to G, "What happened to Alexandra?"

"I'll tell you later. No big loss."

"That's for sure."

G is irked by that comment. And the fact that Kate was right all along, irks him even more.

Everyone is seated now. Wine is flowing, appetizers are arriving, and guests are laughing.

Kate hands G an envelope. "This is for you."

He smiles as he accepts the envelope, teasing, "Looks a little small to be a Porsche."

She laughs and says, "The Porsche wasn't going to make it in time, so I went a different route. It's a gift certificate for dance lessons."

Sydney is sitting next to them, listening in on their conversation. She shrieks in delight at the idea of dance lessons. "Ooh! Sounds like fun!"

However, G is quick to reassure Sydney. "She's just kidding. She knows I don't need lessons. I'm a natural."

Kate rolls her eyes but smiles at G. "You're something alright. It's tickets to a Yankees game."

"Hopefully you're kidding," G replies.

"Why don't you open it and find out."

"Where's the fun in that?" G winks at Kate. She winks back at him, surprising him. "When did you learn how to wink?"

"I learned quite a few things these past weeks." She looks at Luca with a smile. "Would you like to know what else?"

"That's okay. I don't think my virgin ears can handle all the details." G finally gets around to opening the envelope. "Oh, wow!"

Sydney struggles to look over his shoulder. "What is it?"

"Tickets to the Tim McGraw concert. That's awesome! Thank you." He puts the envelope in his jacket pocket and directs his conversation to Luca.

"So, Luca, last night here, huh? You must be excited to get home."

Luca reaches for Kate's hand. "Not so much. I have had such a wonderful time with Kate these past days, but I know she needs to write, and my boss is starting to wonder when I am to return to work."

"But we will see each other in Vienna in a few months," Kate interjects.

G is puzzled at Kate's announcement but decides to skip over the topic. He looks at his watch and wonders out loud, "What could be keeping my parents? As soon as they get here, we will get dinner going."

"It's not like your mom to be late. I could freshen up a bit anyway. Excuse me."

"I'll go with you," Sydney says, rising to join her.

Just before Kate leaves the table, she mouths "Be nice" to G and nods her head in Luca's direction.

Once the ladies are out of the room, G turns away from the others to talk directly to Luca. All pretense of civility has gone out the window. "You weren't supposed to come back with her," he growls.

Luca expects this. "I know."

"And you certainly weren't supposed to have sex with her. Boy Scout promise, remember?"

"I know. I do not know how anyone could resist her. You would have to be an idiot," Luca shoots back at G, clearly aiming that last comment at him. G does not appreciate that.

"And what's this crap about Vienna? I'm not paying for that."

"I do not expect you to. And I will be returning to you the money for the cruise. I do not know what to say. She is nothing how you describe her to me. Sneaky sexy, *si*. I find her to be when I first meet her. Then once I get to know her, I realize what an amazing woman she is. I think I do not have to tell you that."

"Yes, she is, and I would hate to see her hurt."

"Then why do you want her to stay as she is, when she clearly is ready to adventure out into the world on her own? I know you wanted for me to show her a good time and dance, but if you really knew her, you would know she yearns for so much more."

G's parents arrive at that moment, sparing Luca G's intended response. Both men stand to greet them properly. Seeing Luca, G's mom smiles widely and hugs him tightly. She starts talking rapidly in Italian, excited to see him at the party. This upsets G, who reminds her in Italian, "Mom, you are supposed to pretend you don't know Luca, remember?"

She gives G a look of displeasure, but listens to him.

Meanwhile, in the ladies' room, Sydney stands at the sink, touching up her makeup. Kate comes out of the stall to wash her hands, just in time to see Sydney lighting a joint. She watches in surprise and interest, never having seen this in person.

Sydney notices Kate staring at her. "Oh, I'm sorry," she says hurriedly. "Here, help yourself."

"I, uh...I never...I mean, I don't know exactly what to do."

"Oh, here, like this." Sydney demonstrates, then hands the joint to Kate, who takes a puff. And promptly coughs. "We better get back. Take one more."

Kate obliges, coughs again, and returns the joint to Sydney, who finishes it and flushes the remains down the toilet. She pulls a bottle of perfume from her purse and sprays Kate and herself. "Covers up the smell."

Kate and Sydney return to the party. When she realizes that G's parents have arrived, Kate rushes to embrace them. She is happy to see them and introduces Luca, who is greeted warmly. Sydney, on the other hand, is received frostily by G's mom when he introduces the woman.

They return to their seats and begin talking while the waiters come to take the dinner orders.

G looks at Sydney and Kate, his eyebrow raised. "I was about to send out a search party. You two okay?"

Kate is the first to speak, and the effects of her first-time marijuana use are evident. "Oh yes; we are j-u-u-u-st fine," she giggles.

Luca touches her arm and asks her again, "Are you sure you are okay?"

Sydney tries to head off the questions. "She's fine. We're fine." She realizes that Kate may have overdone it a bit. She pushes the basket of bread in front of Kate and points to the water glass. Kate downs the contents of the glass and pulls a few pieces of bread onto her plate.

"Kate, how's Chelsea?" G asks. Kate turns to respond but says nothing, just stares at him. G waves at her, hoping to interrupt the blank stare. "Hello? You in there?" Kate waves back but still doesn't say anything. Sydney pushes another glass of water in front her.

Luca strokes her arm, "Kate? Kate?"

She turns to him like she has never seen him before. "Well, hello! Aren't you handsome?"

Kate looks puzzled about something and turns to Sydney. "My voice sounds funny, doesn't it? Does it sound funny to you? La-la-la!"

Now Kate breaks out into uncontrollable laughter. She tries to whisper to Sydney, but it's not much of a whisper. "I think my voice sounds funny when I'm high. Oh, shoot!" She leans into Sydney. "Oops, I think the jig is up."

Luca laughs. "I think the jeeg was up a while ago." He finds this funny; however, G is mad. "Sydney, what did you two do in the ladies' room?"

Sydney giggles and observes, "You said 'doo-doo'!"

Luca is still chuckling. "Looks like you can cross another thing off your list." He reaches for Kate's hair and brushes it behind her ear.

G doesn't find this amusing at all. "I did not say 'doo-doo'! I said 'you two.'"

"You just said it now!" Kate and Sydney are hysterical at this point. They high-five each other and laugh loudly, causing the rest of the guests to look at their antics without understanding what's happening.

By this time, Kate has finished three glasses of water. She stands up from her chair and says, "I have to use the restroom again."

Sydney starts to get up. "I'll come—"

G stops her. "No, you won't."

"Oh, G; you're such a party pooper."

Sydney huffs but sits back down. Luca watches Kate walk to the restroom. She comes back just as the food arrives. Not realizing how hungry she is, she begins to eat and drink more water. Her case of the munchies disappears as she slowly returns to her normal self.

As the party winds down, some of the guests start to leave. The owner comes out to say goodbye to G and his parents. Kate stands up and walks over to G. "Sorry about the giggles. Happy birthday. Hope you had a nice time."

Luca joins them and pipes in, "*Si, buon compleanno,* Giacomo."

Sydney is confused at hearing the unknown name and looks between the two men. "Who's Giacomo?"

Kate is equally confused. "That's G's full name. How did you know that?" she asks Luca.

"I...I, uh, must have heard someone call him that," he replies lamely. Changing the subject, he says, "Well, shall we head out? I will get the car and meet you out front. *Buonanotte tutti*!"

With a wave, Luca is out of the room. As the crowd thins, G's mom approaches Kate.

"Ah, now I see the reason for that smile on your face. And it makes me happy. I always hoped that one day, you and my Giacomo would find your way to each other. But he's not so smart sometimes."

"You're sweet, Mrs. Amici. G is a good friend."

"Yes, well, come see me next week; we'll cook."

"I'd love to. Bye, Mrs. Amici."

Kate turns to Sydney. "Nice to meet you, Sydney."

"Yes, nice to meet you too. You're not as scary as I thought."

"Excuse me?"

"I met Adriana last week. You remember her? She dated G awhile back." Kate definitely doesn't waste time remembering the women who come and go in G's life. Sydney senses this and continues, "Anyway, she warned me about you. No one measures up to Miss Perfect Kate."

Still confused, Kate is about to ask her to explain when G comes over. "Okay, ladies. Stop all the talk about how wonderful I am. Kate, go home and write."

"Yes, sir!" She gives him a salute, then a hug and a kiss. She then turns to Sydney and hugs her warmly before waving to the remaining guests and heading for the door to find Luca.

TWELVE

The next morning, Kate and Luca are driving to the airport. It's quiet. Kate is focusing on driving, and Luca is looking out the window. The contrast between the night before and this moment is stark. They made love then held on to each other all night long. Kate woke up in the arms of her lover, a smile gracing her face as she tried to soak in every inch of him, to make sure she would remember this feeling. Kate relished having his arms around her. She felt safe and loved. And Luca, for the first time, gave his entire being to someone without fear.

Their arrival at the airport causes a swell of strong emotions for both. They know it's time to say goodbye. Vienna is but a distant promise as each lover tries to sort through their feelings in the here and now.

Kate pulls the car into the garage and finds a place to park. Luca gets his suitcase out of the trunk. Inside her head, Kate is screaming, "Please don't go!" But for some reason, the words won't come out. It's all for the best, she tells herself. At this very moment, she is sad about her time with Luca coming to an end, but equally excited about what the next few weeks and months have in store for her. This is new territory for her, and for once, she is going to embrace rather than question it.

They walk, hand in hand, across the parking lot and into the terminal. The next minutes are spent with Luca checking in and dropping off his luggage. Then they walk across a large area on the way to the security checkpoint. Couples and families are saying goodbye to departing passengers, while exuberant people are hugging those arriving.

Kate and Luca hear the sound of music as they enter the wide-open space. Sure enough, there's a man playing the piano beautifully.

Before getting in the security line, Luca veers off to the side, holding Kate's hands lightly while facing the woman he has come to know and respect. He lowers his forehead until it touches hers. She throws her arms around him and hugs him tightly.

The piano man starts a new song, "If You Asked Me To." The lyrics sum up their emotions.

Used to be that I believed in something
Used to be that I believed in love
It's been a long time since I've had that feeling
I could love someone
I could trust someone
I said I'd never let nobody near my heart again, darlin'
I said I'd never let nobody in
But if you asked me to
I just might change my mind
And let you in my life, forever
If you asked me to
I just might give my heart
And stay here in your arms forever.

Kate and Luca sway a bit to the music, then lean in to share the sweetest kiss ever between two people at an airport. She loosens her grip. They step back. It's time to go. Luca picks up his carry-on bag and steps into the security line. With tears rolling down her cheeks, Kate watches him disappear into the crowd.

~

For the next five days, Kate writes feverishly. She barely comes up for air. She ignores her cell phone except for texts from Luca. He made it back home and missed her the minute he got on the plane. Going back to work only reminds him of the night they met, making him think of her even more.

He enjoys hearing about her progress, and she enjoys sharing it with him. Her stories have taken on a more sensual nature, not as vivid as she thought they would be when she set down to write them. Her night at the club in London is the final story and is more descriptive than the rest. In it, her female character stays and enjoys an amazing tryst with the hot DJ—something Kate wishes she had been brave enough to try. Still, she feels it all worked out for the best.

She has truly found the clarity she was looking for and, in the process, has found her voice. No more pretending to be something she isn't. Less wishing things were different and more making it happen. Less plotting and planning, more living in the moment and going with the flow.

Finally, she types "The End" and hits "Print." While the printer does the magic of putting her thoughts on paper, Kate takes a shower, slips into a flirty dress and heels, and adds a touch of lip gloss. It's definitely a departure from her look of just a few weeks ago. She grabs the manuscript hot off the printer and heads to the station to catch the next train into the city. She wants to get to G before lunch.

G's office is located in one of the tallest skyscrapers in New York. The whole elevator ride up, her stomach is growling. She now realizes that she has barely eaten or slept in the last five days.

The elevator stops on his floor and she steps out. Kate walks straight into his office, not stopping to ask his secretary if G is busy. She drops *Sleep Naked* on his desk with a thud.

"There."

G looks at her, picks up the manuscript, and reads a few pages from the middle. "Looks like your adventure on the cruise really helped. This is good."

Kate reaches into her bag and pulls out another manuscript. She waves the bound copy in the air before dropping it on his desk with another thud. G looks at her with surprise. He picks up the book, whose title is written in big, bold letters on the first page.

"*The Proper Kiss*? You wrote another book?"

"I did. It just flowed, so I kept going. Now I'm tired and starving, so will you please take me to lunch?"

G raises his eyebrows, gets up, puts on his coat, but doesn't head to the door.

"So, now that your boyfriend is gone, I'm guessing you'll be back on the prowl."

"First of all, he's not my boyfriend, but he is very special to me. And I really don't understand your attitude toward him. Can we just go eat lunch, please?"

Her lack of sleep is making her less willing to discuss Luca with G. They walk in silence past the other attorneys and out the main lobby door to the elevator.

"So, you're not a couple? You guys looked pretty cozy from what I could see."

"He's back in London. I'm here. We had a nice time together—and I mean a *really* nice time—but it is what it is for now, so that's that."

She realizes her statements are not making any sense but doesn't care at the moment. Her relationship with Luca is not up for discussion, especially with G.

"Well, I'm glad you came to your senses."

The elevator arrives, and G gets in. Kate is still standing in the lobby.

"Came to my senses? Really? I would think you'd be happy for me, but no!"

"Are you coming?" He has his finger on the hold-open button.

Kate walks into the elevator in a huff. "Only because I'm hungry."

G looks at her. Clearly agitated, she barks, "What's your problem now? Why are you looking at me that way?"

G exhales slowly and releases the hold-open button. As the door closes, he backs Kate against the wall. She drops her bag in surprise, as well as with a slight expectation of where this will lead. G caresses Kate's face, a gentle act compared to his next one. He angles his knees to spread her thighs and glues his body to Kate's heaving form. G takes her hands and pins them against the wall, looking like he wants to devour her. Kate closes her eyes in anticipation as he leans closer still, leaving no space between their two bodies. He tentatively brushes his lips against hers, and soon it becomes a proper passionate kiss—in an elevator.

A few weeks later, Claudia and Kate are spending a much-needed girl's day together.

"*Sleep Naked* turned into a collection of sensual short stories inspired by none other than Signor Luca Bell'Angelo," Kate explains. "*The Proper Kiss* is my story. I changed the names to protect the innocent, of course."

They both laugh.

"Spill!" Claudia demands. "What happened with G after the elevator?"

"We just looked at each other, walked out of the elevator, had lunch, and didn't talk about it. Not a word. At one point, I thought I'd imagined it. Lunch was surprisingly nice. We talked about plans for contacting a publisher. It turns out he remembered a friend who knew someone who knew someone who worked at a big-name publishing house."

"Wait, that was it?"

"After lunch, he called for his car service to bring me home. He opened the door, held my hand, kissed me on the lips, and lingered a bit. When he pulled away, he was just looking at me, smiling."

Claudia looks at her best friend, shock evident on her face. Again, she confirms, "So *that* was it?"

"Until about a week later. He called to tell me he had set up a meeting with the publishing company that was interested in my books. He wanted me to meet him and the company rep for dinner."

"I *knew* there had to be more to it. Keep going!"

"The meeting was great. They asked what else I had, and I told them some ideas. G told the guy he would review the contract the next day, but everything looked good. The guy was happy. He said he was looking forward to working with us, and he left. It was just me and G at the restaurant. G ordered a bottle of champagne, and we toasted to my new career."

"Oka-a-a-ay, this is getting good!"

"Then he told me he didn't like the ending to *The Proper Kiss*—that Maria, my main character, and her agent, Leo, should have had sex. I told him endings could be rewritten, but since he was the one who told me to write what you know....Well, we barely made it to his apartment. It was incredible."

Kate is reliving the evening in her head and lets little details slip to Claudia as she remembers the walk back to his apartment.

They both know what is coming and pick up the pace. Once inside, G pulls Kate toward him and kisses her with such passion she could have had an orgasm just from that.

Sensing her pleasure, he says, "Not so fast," leaving her wanting as he pulls away. They walk into the living room, G heading to the bar to fix them a drink. Kate, practically salivating at the thought of what is happening, sits on the couch in her best come-hither pose. They don't take their eyes off each other, relishing this moment for what it is—the long-anticipated coming together of two people who have been attracted to each other for many years.

As G starts to walk over to her, Kate rises and walks to his bedroom, turning to stop in the doorway and look over her shoulder. He follows her to find her sitting on the edge of his bed. He stops and stands in front of her, handing her a glass of wine she promptly puts on the floor next to her. It is now her turn to drive him crazy. She unbuckles his belt, unzips his pants, and untucks his shirt. Lowering his pants and briefs, she grabs his penis and tugs on it to bring him closer. She licks up one side and down the other before taking him into her mouth as far as she can, sucking ever so slowly, lingering at the tip and then going in far again. There are sounds coming from him that she has never heard him make, and that turns her on. She stands up and pulls off her dress to expose a light purple satin bra and matching panties. He steps out of his pants and drops his shirt to the floor.

"You have too many clothes on," he whispers in her ear as he slides one hand under her hair and around to the back of her neck before pulling her to him. Their kiss is deep, wet, and long.

Fumbling to remove her bra and panties, G stops long enough to admire the woman he is about to devour. He fondles her breasts, she grabs his penis, their mouths exploring every inch of the other. Their growing excitement cannot be contained any longer.

G lays her on her back on the bed, roughly pulling her forward toward him as he stands at the edge. Looking down at her, he teases her wet pussy with his now rock-hard penis.

Kate is writhing with ecstasy as he wraps his arms around her legs and enters her. Kate is clawing at the bedspread, unable to contain herself, and cries out, "Oh my God! O-h-h-h-h-h-h my God!" as the pace of his thrusts quickens.

As her body convulses from the intense orgasm she just experienced, G thrusts one last time before he comes, moaning, breathless. Still inside, he lowers to kiss her, then collapses on the bed next to her.

Not telling Claudia all of the intimate details, she sums up the evening for her friend with, "One intense night of sex like I never imagined."

"So now what? Does Luca know?"

"Let's just say I am going to do a little sexploring for a while. I, well, I mean DD Meloni; that's my pen name. Luca gave it to me. It means double D melons! Anyway, DD started a blog: *Sexplorations*. I really don't know what's going to happen. And I'm more than okay with that. I like spending time with G for sure, and I just bought my ticket to Vienna for New Year's Eve."

Claudia soaks up every word while they finish their lunch. "I see your wishbone necklace is gone. When did that happen?"

"The night G and I met the publisher and had sex."

"So, what was it, getting the book deal or sex with G?"

"I wish I knew. I just noticed it was gone. Not sure when it broke, but it was that day."

Claudia sits back in her chair. "So where do you go from here?"

"I've got to get busy on the sequel. They want it like yesterday."

"Have you thought about it yet?"

"As a matter of fact, I know how I want it to start. Maria finds out that her agent, Leo, paid the hot young guy to meet her on the cruise."

"Ooh, what a twist! Love it!" Claudia takes a sip of her drink and asks, "How do you come up with these ideas?"

"Because that really happened. G found Luca somehow and paid him to meet me on the cruise, to keep an eye on me. He thought the dancing would distract me from having a one-night stand. He made Luca promise hands off."

"You're serious? Oh my God; how did you find out?"

"There were clues all along that I missed, but then one thing happened that solidified it for me. Then it all made sense."

She smiles at Claudia and leans back in her chair, fully expecting her friend to hit her with a million and one questions.

ACKNOWLEDGMENTS

My family and friends are a main reason this book is in your hands. Thank you to my daughters, Lauren and Samantha, and my in-laws, Rosemary and Alex, for always supporting me and my dreams. Kevin and Grace Cover, thank you for your constant encouragement. Thanks to Christina, James, and Jennifer Falcone for your votes of confidence. Special thanks to Tina Brennan for reading every version and giving me your feedback.

Scott Benton, I wouldn't be at this point without your insight and direction. Thank you for taking the time to listen and advise. Georgio Valentino, my knight in shining armor! You saved my grammatically incorrect butt and made me write faster than I ever thought I could. Marlene Dryden, you are super talented, and need to write your own story. Thank you for coming to my aid.

To everyone involved with When Words Count, a million thanks! Steve Eisner, thank you for starting this all and assembling a wonderful group of mentors. Athen Desautels, thanks for your steady guidance and keeping us all sane. Gregory Norris, you are an amazing writer and person. Thank you for your honest opinions and copious notes. Andrea Mosier, Jenn Chapman, Flo Korkames—the best "competition" I could have asked for. Four fabulous writers—we made WWC history! Marilyn Atlas and Steve Rohr, I will always value your advice. Tisha Morris, thank you for looking out for me. I am grateful for your help.

To everyone at Woodhall Press, especially David LeGere, I have been waiting my entire life to talk about "my publisher," and I am thrilled that I landed at your doorstep. Thank you for your support and guidance and, above all, your patience with a newbie.

Last, but certainly not least, Dan Socci, thank you for the daily "Did you write?" texts, talking me off various ledges, your creative comments, all the times you make me laugh, and, above all, being the best friend/manager a gal could ever want. You were instrumental in making this a reality. Your Ferrari is on the way.

It truly is the people you meet on the journey that make the journey so special.

ABOUT THE AUTHOR

Lorraine Cover, a fan of all things romance, includes some steamy sex in her debut novel, *Life After Love*. In addition to writing, Lorraine loves ballroom dancing, traveling around Italy, and cooking. She was a finalist in the 2022 When Words Count Manuscript Contest. Lorraine lives in Jacksonville, Florida, with her husband and rescue pup, and is currently working on short stories as well as the sequel to *Life After Love*. Check out LorraineCover.com for the latest news!